Levels to this Shyt 2

Ah'Million

2

Lock Down Publications and Ca$h Presents

Levels to This Shyt 2

A Novel by *Ah'Million*

Ah'Million

Lock Down Publications
P.O. Box 944
Stockbridge, Ga 30281
www.lockdownpublications.com

Lock Down Publications
Like our page on Facebook: Lock Down Publications @
www.facebook.com/lockdownpublications.ldp
Cover design and layout by: **Dynasty Cover Me**
Book interior design by: **Shawn Walker**
Edited by: **Jill Alicea**

Stay Connected with Us!

Text **LOCKDOWN** to 22828 to stay up-to-date with new
releases, sneak peaks, contests and more…
Thank you!

Submission Guideline.

Submit the first three chapters of your completed manuscript to ldpsubmissions@gmail.com, subject line: Your book's title. The manuscript must be in a .doc file and sent as an attachment. Document should be in Times New Roman, double spaced and in size 12 font. Also, provide your synopsis and full contact information. If sending multiple submissions, they must each be in a separate email.

Have a story but no way to send it electronically? You can still submit to LDP/Ca$h Presents. Send in the first three chapters, written or typed, of your completed manuscript to:

LDP: Submissions Dept
P.O. Box 944
Stockbridge, Ga 30281

DO NOT send original manuscript. Must be a duplicate.

Provide your synopsis and a cover letter containing your full contact information.

Thanks for considering LDP and Ca$h Presents.

Acknowledgements

First and foremost, I'd like to thank God. My family has been such an inspiration. The CEO himself (Cash) for all the support. To the men and women on lock who are supportive as well in spite of the circumstances. The love I get from the females at the Hobby Unit. Pretty P., I'm waiting on ya. B. Giles with them five sons, you better get you some 101. Shawty, priceless, I love yah, baby. Truck D! Okay. And to my brothers, I love y'all and miss you even more. Free Donk and King.

Ah'Million

Prologue

"Tell De'Kari to go get my son," the torn sheet of paper read.

"Tell De'Kari to go get my son," Maine repeated a little above a whisper through squinted eyes. His heart began to pump as fast as an addict who had just snorted an abundance of cocaine. His hands trembled as he attempted to pinch the bridge of his nose.

"Tell De'Kari to get my son," he repeated calmly, peering around. Inwardly, he was far from calm. His eyes were bloodshot red. The sad expression that he had worn upon entering had completely transformed. The demonic glare in his eyes that he now possessed scared the old man. Before waiting around for Maine to explode, the C.O. who delivered the handwritten note quickly got out of Dodge.

***

Syren was in her small cell shaking like a stripper. She knew Maine was about to go berserk. The sirens rang out mere seconds after the thought crossed Syren's mind.

"Rack up! Rack it up!" the C.O. shouted.

Anytime the sirens blared and they were told to rack up, there was either a code red or blue. Red was any form of violence. Blue pertained to anything medical. Syren could hear the lady's radio from where she was standing in the doorway of her cell. The cell was as normal as any other. Graffiti covered the walls and a steel toilet sat in the corner. She had a collage of pictures taped on the inside of her door: Jaclyn, herself, and Sheila.

"We have a code red in the visitation area on the fourth floor," the voice on the other end of the radio announced.

Syren's eyes bucked in fear as she thought about the possibility of Maine losing his freedom on behalf of her infidelity.

"Get in your cell!" the C.O. shouted.

Afraid. Syren jumped back as the C.O. slammed the door shut.

***

Meanwhile, in the visitation area, Maine slung chairs and the empty bowls that were used for inmates to place their snacks in.

"Aaarrgghh!" he hollered at the top of his lungs.

C.O's grabbed him and attempted to restrain him, but he managed to get away. The dark blue YSL shirt he wore was torn at the chest area. He was kicking and cursing and throwing things like a lunatic. The entire visitation area was chaotic. The SRT's, which the inmates referred to them as the "jump out boys", marched in, appearing unfazed by the commotion.

"Look out, Freeworld!" the shortest one leading the pack yelled.

"Fuck you, short shit!" Maine roared back with his chest out, seemingly inviting the men to test his gangsta.

Like a pack of wolves, they all charged Maine at once. The short one was the first guy in arm's reach.

Boom!

Maine dropped him like a sack of potatoes. Before dude's body hit the floor, the other men were on Maine like flies on shit. Maine stood his ground, throwing and taking hits. Seeing that Maine wasn't budging, one of the guys ran and retrieved the fire extinguisher off the wall. He peered around to assure no nosy inmates were in sight.

Clink!

As soon as the metal connected with Maine's forehead, blood slowly trickled down. His body hit the floor and the group of men stomped him out like there was no tomorrow.

Two years later

Syren stood outside the nursing home where she was just informed her mother resided. She blinked away the tears as she marched towards the entrance. To think she had everything planned out, then realizing everything had changed, was quite daunting. A week before her release, she discovered that Angie and Brandon had reunited, so there was no way she would even consider calling Angie, knowing it'd cause strife.

The khaki twill pants she wore were a size too big. She pulled them up by the sides as she walked, but that still didn't stop them from being soaked by the large puddles of water. Instantly, she noticed the cozy setting once entering the nursing home.

"Hi, how may I help you?" the Spanish woman behind the desk asked. Her eyes roamed Syren's body from head to toe, giving her a look of distaste.

"I just got out of prison," Syren stated, reading her expression. "Look, I'm here to see my mother, Sheila Minks."

"Let's see here...she's in room A204. Just show me some identification and you're good to go," she said, flashing her crooked smile.

Syren quickly whipped out her TDCJ card and handed it over.

"Uh, ma'am, I can only accept a driver's license or state ID. This isn't proper validation."

"What type of shit is that? I don't have a state ID. I was just released two hours ago!" Syren blurted.

"I'm sorry, m——"

"I want to see my mother!" she yelled, cutting the lady short.

"I'm about to call security," she spoke through clenched teeth.

"You gon' need them, bitch!" Syren voiced as she walked past the counter towards the rear where the rooms were located. She knew her time was limited, so she began to jog down the semi-dark hallway in search of her mother's room. The desk clerk could still be heard yelling, but Syren kept moving without looking back. Stepping inside the elevator, her heart raced as the thought of returning to prison surfaced.

I don't give a damn. I'm seeing my momma today. She pressed two and watched the elevator shut slowly. "Come on, come on," she chanted loudly, stomping her left foot impatiently in the process. A sigh of relief escaped her lips as the elevator sounded.

Ding!

She swiftly scanned the door numbers as she darted down the hallway.

"201, 202, 203…204." She took a deep breath before twisting the knob and opening the door. However, Syren wasn't prepared for what was next to come.

Boom!

A loud thud sounded throughout the hall as the security guard sent Syren crashing to the floor.

***

Syren

"Get your nasty hands off me! You don't know me!" I yelled at the top of my lungs at the beefy security guard that escorted me out of the nursing home. Apparently during my two year stint, my mother had been checked into a nursing home, unbeknownst to me.

"Ma'am, if you keep resisting, we're going to have to call the police and you'll be arrested for trespassing."

"I'm leaving, dang!" I shot back. I pretended to swipe the dust from my clothes while sneaking glances inside my mother's room.

"Momma?" I managed to whisper once she appeared in the doorway. I stood there awaiting a response before realizing she was looking past me.

"What the fuck?" I thought, scowling, obviously confused

"Excuse me, can you send a nurse up here? I had an accident," she uttered weakly.

"Momma? Accident? What's going on? Momma!"

"Ma'am, let's go." The security guard jerked me in the opposite direction.

My lip trembled as the tears formed in my eyes. My heart raced with fear and anticipation. I just didn't understand what was occurring or what had previously occurred for things to come to this. I needed my ID and I needed it now.

I sat at the bus stop, waiting for the next bus to arrive. Full of dread and concern, my left leg bounced uncontrollably. I tried calming my nerves, but I was too amped. I wanted to hurt someone for admitting my mother to this nursing home. That was black folks' golden rule: no nursing homes; take care of one another. My great grandmother instilled that into me and my cousins at an early age. If I found out one of those motherfuckas was pinching on my mother or spitting in her food I was going to be back in prison.

The tears burned the back of my eyes. I just wanted to let it all out, but that would have to wait. Since so much had changed, I had to find a place to stay. Knowing Maine's mother wouldn't want any dealings with me after all the pain and heartache I caused her son didn't stop me from testing my luck anyways.

The city bus neared. I stepped on and deposited my dollar into the machine, which covered the cost for a one-way. Maine's mother Rhonda stayed just a few minutes away. I needed to see my son and I needed to see him fast. As I walked up the street towards Rhonda's house, I couldn't help but to lower my head, ashamed of the ugly glares I was receiving. Not only were my clothes extra big and ugly, but the neck braids didn't help my appearance at all.

Up ahead, the street was packed.

"Lord," I whispered, hoping like hell that I was just seeing shit and it wasn't a gathering or any sort and if so, that everyone was inside. As I got closer, I could see a galore of cars parked in the driveway and alongside the curb of Maine's mother's house. Spotting the group of people on the porch made me want to turn around, but I had to see Jaelyn. Instantly I noticed Tae, whom I hadn't seen in a year and a half. The sight of her really frightened me. My heart beat rapidly with each step, knowing Maine was somewhere close by. I hated that these bitches had to see me at my worst. Fuck it.

I approached the two-story home with wide open arms and a phony smile.

"Hey y'all!" I yelled to no one in particular.

"Syren?" Tae asked through squinted eyes. Everyone looked surprised and disgusted, but I continued to smile to appear unfazed.

"Hey baby!" I screamed, running up to Jaelyn and wrapping my arms around his neck. I missed my baby so much. Little did I know he was rolling his eyes?

"Hey Ma!" he spoke dryly after I released my grip.

I pulled back and stared at him in disbelief. After two years, he still did not miss me one bit. He didn't even try faking it. I looked around ashamed, making eye contact with a few of the people that peered into my direction.

The half-naked thots that attended the gathering, obviously trying to get a couple of dollars and some dick, looked at me in disgust.

"Boo! What you hoes looking at?" I asked, ready to turn up on they asses. They all mumbled something under their breaths and turned to walk away.

"Syren!" I looked up to see Ms. Rhonda peering at me from the porch with her hands on her hip. "It's good seeing you," she mentioned, walking with me inside her home.

"Good to see you, too," I responded hesitantly.

"Now sweetie, I'm happy to see you, but you look like you walked straight from the prison." Ms. Rhonda leaned back and examined me like I was some kind of animal.

"Yes, Rhonda, I was released today about two hours ago."

"Strange. How did you find out about the party? Why didn't you change your c——"

"Look, Rhonda, I don't have shit! Okay, if this is your way of telling me to leave 'cause I don't meet the dress code, fine!" I hopped up to my feet and headed for the door.

Maine happened to be walking in. It had been a minute, but LAWD, did he look good. He had grown a beard - no James Harden shit, but a li'l sexy shadow that was lined up to perfection. Although he wore a simple Nike 'fit, he was dripping from his neck and wrist. The gold trimming around the black Tom Ford shades perfected his entire look.

"Since you are the mother," he stated.

"What happened to my mother, Maine?"

14

"Ask your baby daddy." He smirked and I tried to move past him.

"Like I was saying, Syren, since you're the mother… Let me rephrase that. Since you're Jaelyn's mother, and I love him as if he's my own, you can crash on the couch."

I nodded my head in agreement, thankful for the proposition, as I peered back at the brand new sofas.

"Not those couches, Syren. The one in the basement, bitch."

My left brow ascended while I peered at him like he had shit on his face. "Yo' weak ass got me fucked up. Kiss my ass!" I wanted to tell his mother to kiss my ass too, but I left it at that and stormed out of the house.

Everyone was looking in my direction, but pretended to be doing their own thing once they saw me fly out the door. I was angry and upset. All at once I shot Jaelyn a look, hoping he'd said something, anything, to express his love in some way, but he didn't. I couldn't even say "let's go home". I didn't have a roof over my head or a set of wheels to get around. Like a bitch with no ass, I didn't have shit.

"Hey Mama!" Jaelyn called out.

My heart dropped when I heard his voice. I guess he cared after all. "Yes, Jaelyn?" I answered with a smile.

"You have something red on the back of your pants."

I looked behind me while turning my pants so I could see. I knew I had felt the sharp pains, but I thought it was from the beefy security guard tackling me. Lo and behold, it was cramps. Today couldn't get any worse. Jaelyn looked like he was ashamed for me, yet he said nothing. I didn't even try to hide the stain. I just started in the direction I had come from.

With tear-stained cheeks and aching feet. I sat on the crowded city bus, thinking of my next move. I tried hard not to sneeze, knowing if I did, the stain on my pants would worsen. The tears I held back at Rhonda's house now filled my eyes as I stared bleakly out the window of the bus. I didn't even try blinking them away. I was done trying to mask this shit. Someone else's perception of me was the furthest thing from my mind.

Bing!

The door to the bus slid open and I quickly rose to my feet and descended the steps. I waited for the bus to proceed before crossing the street to the cheap motel. A foul smell assaulted my nostrils. It was me - a mixture of blood and mildew. The puddle of water in front of the nursing home was so deep it nearly touched my kneecaps. I should've taken care of my wet clothes then 'cause I was definitely paying for it now. I kept it moving towards my destination, funky and all.

The cheap bell on the door sounded as soon as I opened it. An elderly man sat reclined on an old, worn out loveseat behind the counter. He didn't even bother to alter into professionalism after spotting me. He simply continued to stare at the nineteen inch flat screen TV.

"Excuse me, sir?"

"It's thirty bucks a night, fifty for two nights, and for every extra night it's an additional thirty bucks."

"I'll take two nights," I requested, retrieving the crumbled bills from my shirt. My hands shook like I had taken the wrong medication when really I was just that upset. Here I was, my first day home. No Sheila, no Jaelyn, not even a bubble bath or home cooked meal. Just a two night stay in a shitty motel.

He slid me the room key and I vanished like a thief in the night. With just forty-eight dollars left, I was going to have to spend very wisely. If prison didn't bless me with anything my entire incarceration, the hundred dollars they gave me at the gate was surely a blessing.

As soon as I pushed the door open to the room, I peered around in disgust. I could see why it was merely thirty bucks. It should've been ten. A mattress sat alone in the corner of the room. No bed frame, box springs, or rails; just a pissy mattress. The corner of the walls were covered in mildew.

"I know damn well this bitch didn't pass inspection," I mumbled under my breath. The roaches didn't run for cover when the door opened and the light seeped in from outside. They strolled, then stopped directly in front of me like this was their shit and I was the intruder. Shutting the door behind me, I tossed the keys on the dresser and began chasing the roaches down like I was an African and they were cheetahs.

After sweeping up and flushing the ones that I killed, I stood in front of the mirror that was above the sink, disgusted with my reflection. I flicked the light switch off and searched the place top and bottom for any form of toiletries. I knew I wouldn't find anything, but I hoped I did.

"Fuck!" I yelled out in frustration, flopping down onto the floor by the toilet. I could feel the blood flowing out of my pussy. I rushed to my feet, pulling down my underwear and pants to examine the stain. It wasn't as bad as I thought, but from now until I made it to the store, it would be. I needed something to slow it down. I quickly peered around, but I got the same results. Sighing while shaking my head, I frowned at the sight of the white Hanes sock peeking from underneath my pants leg. Slowly I removed the cheap loafers and pulled off my sock. I folded it twice, to where it was a little longer and wider than the seat of my panties, placing the semi-dry cloth on the wet seat of my panties. I then pulled them up as far as they could go so the sock would stay in position.

I unlocked the door and peered around the empty room before leaving.

***

Maine

I enjoyed seeing every bit of distress written on Syren's face when I gave her the ultimatum, and I meant every word of that shit too. With all the lies and fuckery, she was lucky to be walking. To find out not only that my son isn't mine but belongs to a dude that's been my friend since grade school? Not only that, but she fucked and got in a relationship with my blood sister Tae. I gave her a pass on that 'cause she caught her cousin Kreesha sucking my dick. It was shortly after I found out about her and Tae, so I felt as if it was done out of spite. The news of my son belonging to another nigga is what really broke me down. If it wasn't for my mental health attorney pleading my case in court, my black ass would've gotten some serious time for assaulting all of those C.O.'s.

During the li'l stint I did locked up, I was informed from my mother that De'Kari had dropped Jaelyn off at her place and left her a couple thousand to take care of any needs while I was away. He ended up contacting me, asking me for forgiveness, and that it was merely a mistake. If I was willing to let bygones be bygones, he'd stay out of my way, which is what he did. He didn't want any parts of the apartment complex and at the time, it was too much for me to deal with on my own, so I sold it. Kept my cut and his. Fuck that nigga, and if I see his ass right now or two years from now, I'm gon' stretch his ass out. Like the Yella Beezy lyrics, I was back at it again. Before anything moved, shit went through me.

"Momma, I'll be back, but remember what I said."

"Leave me alone, Maine, you've told me ten times already. Honestly, I don't want her here at all, not even in my damn basement!"

"Alright, lady. She will be back. She don't have shit. She ain't got no choice but to come back!" I yelled, walking out the door and onto the porch. "You coming with me, J?"

"No, Pop, I'm going to stay over Grandma Rhonda's house," Jaelyn replied, catching then tossing the football to Tae.

I didn't trust my sister, but I left the past in the past for the sake of our loved ones. I chucked the device to a few of my boys and winked at some of the hoes that glanced in my direction while their men had their backs turned before hopping in my ride.

Since closing down shop with managing the apartment complex, I had switched things up and invested my money into something bigger and better - not in a sense of size, but financial gain. It wasn't just a gambling shack. It was designed with a nice

18

stage in the back, and I managed to obtain some of the finest strippers to utilize it.

It was a little before 5 p.m. when I pulled into the lot of my establishment. Mack City, to be exact. It appeared fairly small on the outside, but it was very spacious on the inside.

"Mack Maine! It's a few chicks here to see you. They trying to get down," Jerry said, whispering the last part.

Jerry was the doorman and he handled a few other miscellaneous missions. I tried not to give him too many assignments. I didn't want him to assume he had any relevant position other than the one that was assigned to him. Since the betrayal from my longtime friend De'Kari, I had been moving solo in every aspect. I'd be damned if I let a nigga get that close again.

I dapped up Jerry and proceeded into the shack. It wasn't even five and the place was semi-packed. My office was in the back, where the illegal things were at. The front room consisted of four slot machines, a pool table, craps table, card table, and a few more round tables were set up for multi-purpose. The back is where the main stage was set up. Sometimes it would get so packed dudes would circle up in the corner and get the dice game going. Sometimes I'd do a little side betting, but I wasn't going to do any fading. My office was off to the side in the back. A nice small, cozy, plush setting. Round oak desk, a red suede loveseat, and a few framed pictures of Scarface decorated the walls.

"Follow me." I eyed the young women nonchalantly as they made their way to my office. I opened the door to my office for the three ladies and watched them as they all passed me. My eyes bucked in excitement at their voluptuous bodies, but I quickly gathered my composure before they piqued my interest.

"First things first. How old are you? If any one of you are over the age of twenty-five, you can just wait outside," I spoke loud and clear. That was one thing the fellas loved about Mack City. Young pussy. I had some of the finest tenders walking these Dallas streets, and they all wanted to work for me 'cause they know my spot is the place to be.

"Oh, then we over good 'cause we all under twenty-three," the chocolate one spoke. She had lips like Meagan Good and her bedroom eyes were enchanting. Her skin was the color of the chocolate swirl in the Nutella container. She blew me a kiss after she said that and it made my dick twitch.

"Okay, ladies, I only have room for two for tonight and the rest of the weekend," I announced, watching their shoulders sag. I always told this lie whenever the ladies would come in a group of three or more. Why? Because it turned into a mini competition right inside my office.

"Come on!" the light-skinned one pouted.

"Don't be like that," the brown-skinned one added.

"We're all sisters. We come as a package. So tell us what we got to do so that we'll all get through," the chocolate one spoke up. She spoke with a hint of aggression, yet she possessed an innocence, a charm.

"Get naked."

In one swift motion, the ladies began to remove their clothing, which looked a lot like Fashion Nova.

"Names?"

"Candy Redd, P. Mula, Cocoa."

All of their bodies were like masterpieces.

"Do a 360 and a quick trick to show me you a savage and not average."

"This nigga think it's a game. Come on, y'all," Cocoa said, scrolling down the face of her phone with her fingertips. The music seeped out of her phone at a high volume, loud enough to be heard over the commotion outside of the office.

> I'm a savage
> Attitude ratchet, talk big shit but my bank
> account match it.
> Hood but I'm nasty;
> Rich but I'm classy.
> Haters keep my name in they mouth

Now they gagging…

On cue, the girls turned around, still fully nude, bent over, and grabbed their ankles, making their asses clap to the beat. I was mesmerized by the view of Candy Redd's love button from the angle I was sitting at. They twerked their asses in unison to the Mcgan Thee Stallion beat before dropping down into splits. Cocoa added a little extra to the ending as she bounced up and down a few times. She winked at me right before standing to her feet.

I gotta have her, I thought.

I'd seen my share of dancers. I'd seen bitches twerk, but it looked like they'd been twerking since the womb. These chicks right here made the shit look easy. They could come through and hit Mack City anytime.

"That was cool. I'll see all three of you tonight. Bring ya A game."

"We always do," Cocoa retorted.

"Hey, Candy, P. Mula, y'all dismissed. Cocoa, hang back. I need to holla at you real quick."

***

<u>Syren</u>

The ray of sunshine awoke me from my deep slumber. Even the blinds that covered the windows were raggedy. It seemed as if they had previously been cracked or split as the clear scotch tape held them together. My prison-issued clothes hung over a metallic rail. From where I lay, they appeared still damp. I was hoping they'd dry soon so I could start my day.

"Thank you Lord," I praised aloud. In the midst of it all, all glory goes to God 'cause I could be dead or still behind prison walls being told when to wake up, sleep, eat, and wash my ass. This is far from the best life, but it's the fuckery before the fortune, so I'm not trippin'.

Forgetting I had started my cycle, I raced to the restroom. Flopping down onto the porcelain toilet, I grabbed the maxi pads off the shelf. After purchasing ten dollars worth of hygiene items that I use on an everyday basis, I simply couldn't afford the dollar and eighty-nine cent box of tampons, so I bought two packs of seventy-nine cent pads and just like the days in prison when I had no tampons, I made one with the pad. I peeled off the top layer, set it across my lap, then grabbed a handful of the compacted cotton and formed it close to the size I wanted. Using merely a square of tissue, I folded it in half and then wrapped it around the cotton. Taking the thin but protective layer from my lap, I rolled the cotton in it as tight as I could and tied the rest of the material in a knot, which kept it in place. It wasn't the best, but it had to do.

After rinsing my hands, I felt all over my clothes to ensure they were dry. Some spots were slightly damp yet. I threw the clothes on anyway.

My first mission was to get rid of these lame-ass clothes. While I rode the city bus my first day home I overheard a few young chicks talking about a club called Mack City. Supposedly a bitch could get rich overnight. I didn't do my time like most bitches and gain a hundred pounds. All I managed to gain was six pounds and it went to the right places. The hundred squats a night did me some justice as well. Although you couldn't see it in these clothes, I was stacked.

I entered the Family Dollar, peering around quickly while strolling towards the clothing section. Immediately I spotted the navy blue and black sweat suits. I grabbed the navy blue one and disappeared inside of the restroom before being noticed. I burst into the first stall upon entering and quickly changed into the sweat suit. Once I was dressed, I patted my braids down as if they were out of place. Folding my old clothes up as stealthily as possible, I tucked them underneath the commode. Staring at my reflection in the large mirror, I patted the wrinkles out of my clothes and took off. I pretended to be shopping as I strolled around the store. There was something in particular I was looking for, but I had no plans on buying it.

By this time, the young dark-skinned chick that was positioned behind the register greeting a Hispanic family that was entering the store. The hot pink and black panty and bra set wasn't nothing close to Victoria's Secret, but it was reasonable and cute. I discreetly removed the hanger slowly and watched the cashier watch me. However, she would only see my head peeking out due to the clothing racks I stood on the side of. I slid the bra in between my legs and stuffed the panties on the inside of the panties I wore. Sweat beads formed across my forehead as I peered around the store at all of the cameras. Shoplifting was never my thing, even as an adolescent.

Just one more, I thought.

The red silky-looking camisole and shorts looked sexy and refreshing. I was so intrigued by the simple outfit that I misplaced the cashier. I peered out both corners of my eyes quickly, but there was no luck locating her. At that instant, I slid the shorts under my armpit and the top inside of my bra. I smiled on the inside since I was en route to the door with no one in sight.

"Excuse me, ma'am!"

"Yes?" I turned around, standing face to face with the cashier.

"Did you find anything?" she asked. Her once confident smile turned into a nervous one as I followed her eyes glance down to the bulge in my boobs.

"No. Maybe next time," I lied.

"Okay. Have a nice day."

I flew out the door and down the sidewalk. Whew!

Glancing at my reflection from the side as I bypassed a furniture store, I noticed something small, but certainly visible. As I neared the window, I couldn't believe what I was seeing. The fucking tag on the top I'd stolen was sticking out from the top of my neckline, lying directly on the shirt.

She let me get away, I thought.

I tucked the tag back into the bra and made my way to the beauty supply house, which was just two stores down the strip. If I was going to go pop some pussy, I damn sure was gon' have to look the part, which wasn't going to be a task at all since I had attended cosmetology school and once owned my own shop before my husband – well, soon-to-be husband - found out our son wasn't his.

It was actually his best friend's – ex-best friend's. Speaking of De'Kari, I hadn't spoken to or seen him since the day of my arrest.

As soon as I entered the beauty supply store, the two Vietnamese men shot me an uninviting look. I was going to have to do things in here a little different. I had already devised a plan for my hair for the cheapest but best results. I walked straight towards the braid hair. Just as I expected, the cheapest was a dollar and ninety-nine cents. I grabbed two, but I only intended on paying for one. I then spotted a cheap powder foundation labeled cinnamon by Kiss. I swiped my fingertip across the smooth powder, pressing it against my cheeks. It matched my tone perfectly. I closed the lid and in one swift motion, slid it underneath the sleeve of my sweatsuit.

The concealer was just a buck. *I guess I could pay for it*, I thought. To my left were pallets of blush. I would rather just wear highlights but since they didn't have any, I settled for a L'oreal eyeshadow pallet that contained a shimmery yellow gold, a honey gold, and a shimmery pecan almost bronze color. It was perfect. Since it was priced at $6.99, it would also have to be hidden in the sleeve of my sweater. I grabbed a pair of falsies number sixty-two, a small container of bonding glue, and a pair of stud earrings, the ones that resembled pearls. I approached the counter with just one bag of hair and the concealer.

"Can I get one of those brown eyeliners, a personal blade, and a tube of that lip gloss right there." I pointed as if money wasn't nothing. If only they knew, the three items I requested were a dollar apiece, leaving me with a $7.12 tab.

It was time to show out. I couldn't wait to get back to my motel room.

***

I strutted towards the door of the popular club I had heard so much about, but from the outside looking in, it didn't look as appealing as it sounded. I used my room key and lightly tapped on the door.

"Bossman here?" I asked, trying to peer past him. Certainly confused, I took a step back and looked up at the sign on the door once more.

"What's wrong, baby girl? Bossman in the back. Come on."

I hesitantly followed his lead while taking in the setting. Men and women were gathered around at different tables. Three older ladies occupied the slot machines. I blew out a breath of frustration as my shoulders sagged in defeat. I had come all the way to the other side of town and the place iwas a fucking gambling shack.

Maybe I'll try my luck on one of the slot machines, I thought. I continued to peer around aimlessly while the big guy opened the door that led to the back.

"Come on."

I was so caught up watching the dude with the pool stick in his hand that I didn't hear the guy behind me.

"Hey ma, come on!"

"Shit. I'm sorry," I apologized, following him through the door. My eyes lit up like a kid in a museum once I spotted the huge metallic stage. It may have been empty, but I glared at it like it was full of nude dancers.

"I got someone out here to see you, boss!"

"Give me one second!"

The voice sounded familiar, but I quickly dismissed the speculations.

"Hey, just a heads up, he's going to want to see some skin, ma."

"That's fine," I assured him.

The door to the office opened and my eyes bucked in awe. Maine and Un'Nija came tumbling out of the office. Maine was in the process of buttoning up his shirt, while Un'Nija patted and finger combed her bundles. All movement ceased once they spotted me.

The nerve of this hoe Uh'Nija to glare at me distastefully like Maine wasn't mine first - for twelve years.

"I see that ass whooping wasn't enough," I blurted impulsively.

"Doing all that time away from your mother and child wasn't either, huh?" She grinned.

I gritted my teeth at the bitter remark. I wanted so badly to go upside her head again, but Lord knows I didn't want to reap the consequences. "It's no use arguing with you. You a pussy. You're not going to fight and then when I pop you and fold ya ass up, you going to run me in to the law," I stated sharply.

"Girl——"

"Uh'Nija, chill, damn. What's up? What are you doing here, Syren?" he asked, cutting Uh'Nija short.

I'd be lying if I said I wasn't ashamed. I was. The last thing I wanted to do was fix my mouth to say it in front of this hoe.

"Give us a few minutes, Uh'Nija. Matter fact, I'll just hit you up on my way home," Maine suggested.

Uh'Nija peered at him as if he was speaking in Chinese, but she knew not to speak on it.

As soon as she was out of earshot, I followed Maine into his office. He peered at me through narrow slits until I finally decided to speak up.

"Maine, I want to dance. I need the money."

"Dance? Strip?" he inquired, raising his eyebrows at my statement.

"Yes!"

"Oh, okay, you can dance, Syren. Just not here. Take your old ass down the street. The dancers in here are between the ages of 18 and 25," he replied, shuffling through the paperwork, ignoring my murderous gaze.

I inhaled deeply before speaking while trying to mask my anger. "I might not be twenty-five, but bitch, I ain't old. The bitch that had you is old." In an instant, I snatched my sweatpants down, exposing the lime green lace boyshorts that covered only half of my juicy ass before strutting out of the office.

Feeling like a man who just lost his pitbull, I pulled my pants up as I dragged towards the exit. As I bypassed the pool table, me and the handsome dude that was in the exact spot minutes ago made eye contact. I was about to flash a smile to let him know I was game when I heard Maine call my name.

"Syren!"

"What, Jermaine?"

"Don't handle me like I'm some type of peasant. I don't want your bum ass. Ya son do!" he yelled, flashing his expensive and latest iPhone.

I know his lame ass was trying to embarrass a bitch. I strutted towards him, adding a little extra hip to my twist, since all eyes were now on us. I snatched the phone out of his hand, but the menacing look in his eyes sent chills down my spine. "Hey, baby boy, how are you? I miss you so much."

"Hey Ma," he said dryly. " Ma, I was calling to see if you could sign these papers so I could go to Driver's Ed?"

The smile I had plastered across my face slowly faded once I realized there was a legitimate purpose for his call. "Sure, baby. I'll meet you at your Grandma Rhonda's house tomorrow."

Click!

No goodbye, see you later, or nothing. I slowly handed Maine the phone. On the brink of tears, I rushed out of the club.

***

Tae

I'd been thinking about Syren since the day I saw her. I just couldn't expose the feelings that I buried long ago because I told myself I wouldn't go that route with her again. I smirked the day she walked up the driveway. In spite of the prison clothes, no makeup, and the dookie braids, she was still beautiful. After seeing her emotionless son and her arguing with Maine, I detected the distress immediately, on top of the embarrassment from ruining her clothes. Two years ago I would've opened fire on everybody who spoke on her or laughed. I loved her that much - or so I thought. I

27

bobbed my head as I listened to the lyrics that soothed yet confused my spirit.

> Truth is, I never got over you.
> Truth is, wish I was standing in her shoes.
> Truth is, when it's all said and done,
> Yes, I'm still in love with you.
> Truth is, I never should've let you go.
> Truth is, it's killing me
> 'Cause now I know when it's all said and done
> Yes, I'm still in love with you.

Although me and Maine weren't trying to kill each other anymore, I didn't give a fuck about him or his feelings. If I wanted Syren, then that's what I was going to do, but she had played a nigga to the left. On top of that, me and Iesha were back at it. Iesha holds the key to my heart, but I can't deny I cut for Syren like a motherfucka too. Both women in my life would be perfect. One without the other, I'd be incomplete. Choosing was the hardest thing I've ever done, but Syren left me no choice.

The love I have for Jaelyn sort of eased the hatred I had for Syren. For some reason, Jaelyn wasn't affectionate with Syren at all. Then again, he was at the age where he thinks he's grown.

"Hey, you talk to your mom?" I asked Jaelyn as I turned to face him while we both sat on the hood of my Impala.

"Yeah. My daddy didn't have all the information I needed to fill out the driver's ed application, so when he saw her, he called me then passed her the phone."

"She doesn't have a phone?" I frowned in disbelief.

"No, I guess not."

I sighed while imagining how difficult things were for her. As bad as I didn't want to get involved, it sure was tempting. I began to wonder where she was, being that her mother was in a nursing home.

Ring! Ring! Ring!

"Yo!" I yelled into the receiver. I had been waiting on this call all day.

"Meet me at my spot. Everything in position," De'Kari voiced before hanging up.

Click.

"Aye, li'l Jaelyn, I'm 'bout to go handle something. I'll be back," I uttered while hopping off the hood and dashing to the driver's seat.

"Can you drop me off at Monty's house?"

"You don't think it's too late?"

"Nah. I'm always over there playing 2K."

"Bet, come on."

After dropping Jaelyn off, I sped to meet up with De'Kari. In spite of what happened with me and Maine as well as him rightfully being Jaelyn's father, it didn't harm or alter our bond. Since losing part ownership of the apartment complex, we been chasing the bag ever since.

"She's down the street in the townhomes," De'Kari voiced as soon as I slammed the car door shut.

"You ready?" I asked, peering up at him.

"Yeah, let's do this." We hopped in his all-black GMC. I let the window down and hit the alarm on my Impala.

"It's three dudes in there. They working for some new out of town nigga. The spot is in his bitch's name. You probably don't know her, but her name is Stacy. She thirsty and ratchet. Everyone knows her rep, so she had to cop her a out of town nigga."

"Nah, I don't know her. But do Bunz have her strap on her?"

"Well, since she posed as a stripper bitch, more than likely she half-naked. She has it with her, but I'm not sure if it's in reach."

"It's alright. It just means we have to definitely be on point."

He pulled into the townhomes, parking in the closest parking spot.

"We going around back. The kitchen door is unlocked."

"Bet. Let's do this."

A few people in the townhomes were out and about, appearing to be on their way someplace else. No one was just sitting on the stoop or porch waiting for some sort of entertainment. The golden opportunity.

At a normal pace, we walked towards the townhome, then veered to the left, where we took the dirt path on the side of the townhome that led to the back door.

"All this fucking mud back here, I should've worn my boots," De'Kari whispered. "You ready, nigga?" he continued.

"I'm always ready."

With a twist of the knob, De'Kari slowly opened the door. Moans filled the townhome. Crouched slightly, we tiptoed in the direction of the noise, guns in hand. I constantly licked my lips the closer we got. It's something that I do when I'm concentrating.

From the entryway we gawked at the obscenity displayed before us. Hidden on each side of the door, I watched the three men sexually utilize Bunz. The guy with the dreads stood in front of her receiving oral sex while Bunz bounced and rocked on the penis of the guy that lay underneath her. The chubbier one stood off to the side stroking himself. It appeared that he was waiting for his turn.

De'Kari called Bunz's phone. It was a signal to let her know we were inside. The Yung Dolph and Meagan Thee Stallion lyrics blared through the living room. She reached up and palmed the guy with the dread's ass cheeks while speeding up her pace as she rode the other guy like a cowgirl. That was our cue. We rushed in like SWAT during a drug bust, guns drawn on all three of the men. They all wore the same terrified and surprised expression. All movement ceased. Bunz still had dick in both holes while the dude off to the side still had his in his hand.

"I got these three. Take Fatboy with you and find the loot," De'Kari directed while aiming his two twin Glocks at the trio.

"Come on, Chubbs, put ya dick up and take me where the bread at."

"This some hoe shit," he mumbled.

Removing the black bag tucked on the side of my sweatpants, I followed Chubbs to the back. He led us to the restroom. I tightened my grip on the burner just in case he tried something. Flicking on the light switch, he eased the lid off the wash stand, which is the part above the cupboard below. It seemed sort of awkward to me. He reached in and pulled out a Ziploc bag full of neatly-stacked bills combined with two thick stacks. He tossed it to me, and I thought he was done until he tossed another one. My eyes danced in excitement. He peered around while turning around slowly. I was so thrilled at the amount of money I was holding I never saw dude retrieve or pull the Glock until it was too late.

"Kari!" I shouted while ducking, but the bullet hit me in my shoulder. One of the bags of money hit the ground. I fired recklessly three times. So did he. A barrage of gunfire came from the opposite direction, hitting Fatboy twice in the chest, instantly putting him out of his misery. Looking back and seeing that it was Bunz stunned the shit out of me. I knew she was about that life, but I had no clue that she was a killer. That shit was sexy. But I would never be able to get past the ratchet shit she was doing when we first entered.

"Come on," she said, picking up the other bag of money.

Pants wrapped around their ankles, De'Kari had both men gathering the dope. When the guy with the dreads was done he looked at Bunz and said, "I'm going to get you, bitch." As soon as the words left his lips, a shot was fired, hitting him in the head. It burst open like a watermelon, and brain juices went everywhere.

"Bruh, I don't want no smoke. Y'all will never see me again," the last dude reasoned. He was so scared, piss oozed out of his manhood. It was as limp as a dead body.

"Let's go," De'Kari said, leaving him standing in the living room. The three of us rushed to the truck and hopped in.

"Bitch, where you at?" the chick on the other end of Bunz's phone yelled.

" I'm on my way. Meet me at my crib!"

"Dang, Bunz, you better not fuck this up for us."

"Bitch, just be at my crib 'cause I'm on my way."

Click.

"Hey, drop me off at my spot. I got somewhere important to be. I already got dude eating out the palm of my hand." She and De'Kari shared a grin as he busted a U-turn and headed towards Bunz's spot.

***
Maine

Last night was lit. The trio of sisters put almost five grand in my pocket off their tips alone. See at Mack City, bossman Maine gets ten percent of your money earned because the women are guaranteed to make a lot. So you do the math. If the three sisters gave me a total of five grand and I merely got a ten percent cut, that means these bitches made ten G's or better. The show they put on was worth every penny.

Cocoa wasn't trying to come off any of her goods when I invited her into my office for a one-on-one, so tonight I planned on making a different approach.

Syren had been heavy on my mind since she showed up at my office unannounced. She was so beautiful. Prison had really refreshed her. Her blemish free and smooth skin made her look years younger. Her makeup was flawless and her goddess braids were very neat, perfecting her look. Seeing her dampened my mood and angered me all at the same time. I hated the fact she was no longer mine, but then I hated her for what she had done to me. Seeing her strut out of my office with all that ass hanging out had me ready to snatch her up.

Thinking impulsively, I leaped from behind my desk, but in mid-stride, I realized what I was about to do and I came to a halt. I just had to see if she was giving the niggas in the shack a show. Then I remembered that Jaelyn had been trying to contact her. I flew through the door. I had yelled her name in an attempt to cease the thirsty glares from all the men. I wasn't even sure if Jaelyn had picked up yet. Although I didn't want Syren, I honestly didn't want another nigga to have her either.

"Daddy, where you going?" Uh'Nija mumbled, laying on the other side of my bed.

"What's up, Nija?" I asked, ignoring her question. Uh'Nija and I weren't together, but she did have a spot in my life – a spot she didn't have before all of this. We weren't official, but we were damn close to it.

"Where you going?" she repeated

"If I ignored you the first time, it's for a reason," I replied, sliding my feet inside the house shoes.

"Don't you think I have a right to know?" she asked, leaning up on her elbows.

Every time I'd give Uh'Nija an inch, she'd take a mile. Yes, she had great sex and was willing to go to the moon and back for a nigga, but damn, I can't stand for a bitch to breathe down my neck. I fully understood why Syren did it. I don't recall a time in our twelve year relationship that I was faithful. There was always an "Uh'Nija", meaning there was always a bitch willing to play second.

"You're going to find yourself by yourself steady questioning me," I stated, walking towards the shower.

"Oh, 'cause you're going to meet up with that bitch Syren, huh? Whatever happened yesterday when she popped up at ya spot?"

"Uh'Nija, stop while you're ahead."

"Nah, nigga, you owe me at least an explanation!" she hollered, sitting straight up in the bed.

"I'm going to owe you an ass whooping if you don't leave me alone."

"Oh, so it's like that, Maine?" she asked, peering at me through narrow slits as she slid out of the bed, exposing her voluptuous body. Both hands on her hips, she awaited my response.

I looked at her from the bathroom and began to brush my teeth.

"Cool, I'm going home, but just know I'm not sharing you with her again. Y'all had y'all thing. It's about us now." She raced around my bedroom gathering her belongings.

I watched her out of the corner of my eye, hoping she'd just leave in peace.

"Maine, for the last time. Where are you going?"

I spit into the sink, then wiped my mouth with the back of my hand. "Bruh, if I don't answer you, it's because I don't care to answer you. If I don't care to secure you, that means I don't give a fuck about your feelings, and if I don't give a fuck about your feelings, it has to mean that I don't give too many fucks about you."

"Fuck you too, you ole tender dick-ass nigga," She made clear before storming out.

I wasn't intending on upsetting Uh'Nija, but I hate to explain myself. Even if Syren was on my agenda, it's cool. That was my bitch for twelve years.

I slid into a tank top, Prada jeans, and a pair of my Trans Scott Jordans.

"Jaelyn!" I yelled, grabbing my keys off the dresser.

"Yeah?"

"You ready?"

"Yes sir!"

"Let's go!"

***

Uh'Nija

I raced down the steps and into my car. I was glad Maine had given me a reason to leave.

"Hello?" Tobias picked up. Hearing his deep voice mixed with his Haitian accent made my pussy thump.

"Hey baby, I'm just now leaving my patient's house. I'm on my way home now."

"What happened?"

"She went into a diabetic coma. I contacted her family and waited for them to arrive," I lied, hoping I sounded convincing. After the fallout between me and Syren, it left me no choice but to find work elsewhere. I started doing home healthcare. Between Maine and Tobias, I was spoiled rotten. Being that I didn't need the bread, I quit. I was just using that as a way to spend time with Maine.

"Go ahead and get fresh, then come fuck with me," Tobias instructed.

I grinned like a child who just won a shopping spree. "Okay, daddy."

34

"Bye, baby."

Tobias was just my type. He grinded like he was broke and even though he was so sweet, he played no games. Eventually Maine would have to step up and give me what I wanted or I was going to fall back, and with the way things were going with Tobias and me, leaving Maine's dawg ass wouldn't be hard.

I threw my car into park and hopped out. I took the stairs two at a time. When Maine left the Falls Apartments, so did I. The plush townhome was more of my preference. I stood outside my door twisting and turning as I crossed one leg over the other to keep the piss from flowing down my legs.

"Ooohh, I got to pee," I whispered, pushing my key inside the lock. After hearing the lock click, I burst inside, closing the door behind me and darting to the restroom. "Whew!" I exhaled deeply while relieving myself. That shit almost felt better than an orgasm.

"So is that the type of shit you wear to a patient's house?" Tobias asked, startling the shit out of me.

I nearly jumped off the toilet at the sight of him. I calmed a little after realizing it was just him.

"Tobias! You scared the shit out of me!" I screamed, clutching my chest. I was really trying to think of a lie. He didn't budge or wink. He stood over me, awaiting my response. I wasn't sure if he was already inside or if he had followed me into my spot. I honestly didn't know what to say. "What do you mean work? I was dressed and ready to see you. I got all the way down the street and realized I had to use the restroom. I had been moving so fast to get to you I forgot to pee."

He eyed me skeptically through squinted eyes. In his heart he probably felt that I was lying, but he couldn't prove it. He pulled his phone out and scrolled through his phone. I was terrified of his response as I waited without breathing, shaking like a stripper.

"So...it took you sixteen minutes to get home, get dressed, leave, then double back and pee?"

"Yes, Tobias. I been anxious to see you since the second I left your side. I just want to be in your arms again. I'm an itty bitty bitch. I can get a lot done in five minutes," I lied again.

He stared at me for what seemed like hours. I continued to peer up at him without blinking or looking elsewhere. I didn't want to show him any signs to confirm my lies.

"Alright then. You've never lied to me, Uh'Nija, so I'm going to give you the benefit of the doubt," he said, flashing a slight grin. Although Tobias had a beautiful set of white teeth and sexy lips to go with it, there wasn't an ounce of humor in his eyes. It looked as if someone held a cut-out of a smile up to a straight-faced, emotionless Tobias. It was creepy, yet it made my pussy drip at the same time. I assumed that he'd leave and give me privacy to wipe my pussy, but instead, he pinned his foot against the wall, reclining a bit. I quickly but thoroughly wiped and flushed. His presense was making me feel awkward as fuck. After I rinsed my hands, he followed me out of the restroom.

"You want to just ride with me, or are you going to follow me?" he asked, standing in the living room, watching my every move.

I scanned around quickly trying to grab any kind of hygiene to freshen up a bit, but there was nothing in sight and I didn't want to seem antsy. "I'll follow you, babe. You ready?" I asked in a chipper tone.

"Come on." He opened the door and held it open for me.

My heart raced so fast I was so for sure it would leap out of my chest. I hopped in my Audi and he climbed into his G-wagon. I peered around the backseat, then searched the glove compartment.

"Yes!" I whispered once spotting the baby wipes. Tobias loved sex as much as I did and I knew as soon as we entered his crib he was going to want some of this WAP.

I was dressed in a gray Missoni crop top and matching leggings. I eased them down, then pushed the button that made my engine come alive. Tobias eased out of the parking spot and toward the exit gate of the townhomes. I stayed directly behind him, not wanting him to start making speculations. After exiting the townhomes, we neared the red light up ahead. I prayed it stayed red to give me some time.

I wiggled the leggings down before coming to a stop. Grabbing the bag of baby wipes, I hit the brakes at the light with my left foot, cocked my right leg into the passenger seat, and quickly cleaned my pussy to the best of my abilities. I took another wipe and slid it in between the crack of my ass before rolling down my window. I reached into my Hermes bag and retrieved my Summer's Eve spray. I lightly sprayed my kitty and got back into my driver's position. The light changed and I trailed Tobias smoothly. Minutes later I tossed the wipes out my window and rolled my window back up. My leggings were still down to my ankles as I drove through the streets of Dallas. I scrolled through my phone and deleted Maine's text and call history before blocking his number.

Once we approached another light, I yanked my leggings up. Tears filled my eyes once the thought of calling Kreesha crossed my mind. Her silly ass would've had me laughing at the situation I'd gotten myself in. The thought of not being able to hear her voice dampered my spirit. About a year ago, her body was found in the Trinity River. Her killer was never discovered. Kreesha was loved by many. I don't know what would've possessed anyone to harm her.

I killed the engine after pulling into the driveway of Tobias's two-story house. I checked my bag to make sure I had put the baby wipes and spray inside. I strutted inside, tossing the thirty-two inch bundles behind my shoulder. Tobias's place was always so neat and smelled nice.

"Hey Maria," I spoke upon entering. Maria was his maid and set of eyes all in one. She was about that life. I'm green to a certain extent, but the bulges in her lower back and at her hip were surely noticeable. I've stared at her a few times to see if I can detect any signs that indicate some type of sexual relation between her and Tobias. She wasn't young and she wasn't old, maybe in her late thirties. She wore the attire of a housekeeper, and the only thing that I found appealing were her ocean blue eyes and her long, black wavy hair.

"Hola. U'Nija."

I had tried telling her time after time the correct pronunciation of my name, but time and time again, she fucked it up.

Maria had something similar to a little house a few feet away from the main house. Whenever Tobias and I would arrive, she'd cook whatever we desired from the menu, then disappear to her place.

I walked past Maria and up the stairs that led to Tobias's bedroom. While the two of them were engulfed in conversation, I eased into the restroom that was connected to Tobias's bedroom snatched his towel from the metal rail, ran hot water over it, and wiped my pussy again. I quickly squeezed the water out and placed the towel in the exact spot I found it in. I walked out of the bathroom at the same time Tobias was walking in.

"Maria is cooking one of her five star meals," he said while closing the door behind him.

"I missed you, daddy."

"I missed you too. Show daddy how much you missed him."

In spite of his crazy side, Tobias was perfect. He was handsome as fuck with the perfect touch. I admired his 6'6" frame. His honey-colored eyes were mesmerizing. They almost matched his creamy brown skin. His locs were jet black with honey blonde tips that stopped in the middle of his back. He weighed at least 250 pounds and every time he put that weight on me, I enjoyed every second of it.

I gently pushed him on the bed, then yanked his Polo sweats and briefs down in one swift motion. I worked my way back up and sniffed his sack. "Mmm," I moaned loudly. The fresh smell mixed with a hint of sweat made my mouth water. Instantly I took him inside of my mouth. He lay his head back against the sheets, but suddenly pushed me back.

"You know how I like my dick sucked, Uh'Nija," he stated, standing to his feet. He pulled his shirt over his head then motioned me over. I crawled towards him. "Now get on it," he demanded, gazing down at me with those sexy yet piercing eyes.

I used my tongue to swipe away the pre-cum that had oozed from his penis. Squeezing the base of it tightly, I took him into my mouth while sucking and slurping. His head tilted back as his hands entwined inside my bundles. His thrusts were gentle but noticeable.

"Suck that dick, Nija," he mumbled. He yanked my head back so he could peer into my eyes, then forcefully shoved himself into my mouth. He began to fuck my face while talking that hot shit. His hands locked into my hair as he controlled and limited my movement. I felt the tip of his penis at the back of my throat, but I squeezed my eyes shut and pressed on because I knew this motherfucka wanted to see me choke.

Slobber was running down both sides of my mouth. He began to stroke faster. The width of his massive penis felt as if it was splitting the corner of my mouth, but I was enjoying every second of it. He pulled out, and more of his pre-cum dripped onto my plump breasts. He swiped his dick across my lips.

"Open up," he teased right before ramming all nine inches inside my mouth. I could feel his penis throbbing. I knew he was about to cum. "Aaaargghh!" he roared.

I cupped his balls in one hand as I felt his warm liquid splash the inside of my cheeks.

He grunted, then said, "Damn, girl, I love you. Come on."

Tobias lay me on my side on top of his king-sized bed, then immediately slid behind me. We lay in the spooning position for mere seconds before he rolled me on top of him with my back to him. He slipped his hard dick inside of my creamy kitty and slow-stroked me.

"Ooohh, Tobias," I whispered, biting my lip. He was pulling me down on him as he slowly thrust upward, one hand around my throat and his left arm around my waist. I was in complete bliss while peering up at the ceiling, oblivious to everything else. Tobias began to plant kisses on my neck, deepening his strokes while choking me gently.

He rolled me over on my stomach while still inside of me. Grinding down inside of this pussy with a hint of force compelled my formerly strong build to go as limp as an elderly man's penis in dire need of Viagra. I attempted to throw my ass back, yet his weight made it difficult for me to breathe. I felt held down by an incredible weight disabling my movement. His stiff hard dick ceaselessly drilled into my soul. As he moved his hips from side to side, touching my walls, I tightened my pussy before screaming out, "Tobias! Fuck me, baby!"

A tear escaped my right eye as he grinded inside me cruelly. His penis began to throb, then I felt his hot rush of fresh cum. He collapsed on top of me. He caught his breath, then wiped the single tear away before kissing me softly on my lips. He pulled me on top of him. We were both drenched in sweat as we lay together. His hand slid down and cupped my ass cheek right before I drifted off to sleep.

***

<u>Syren</u>

I licked the envelope before sealing it closed. I had made a vow to my bitches on lock that I'd keep it real. Something so easy, yet a lot of motherfuckas hardly ever do it. No pot to piss in or a window to throw it out of, I still stood on my word.

A smile spread across my face as I thought about RaKeisha and Symphony. I had met RaKeisha as soon as I hopped off the bus. We were both housed at Planestone jail due to the nature of our crimes. Together we pulled up to Mountainview and we'd been friends ever since.

Symphony was a good friend of mine too. Although I had only known her for a short period of time, she was down and cool as fuck. She was realer than most and I peeped it instantly. We clicked like we'd known each other for years. Symphony never admitted it to me, but I know she wanted me in her life - in more than just one way. Symphony never disrespected me or anything I had going, so I never spoke on the irrelevant topic. She was expected to be released next month. I swiped the tears that fell from my eyes after realizing I'd never see Ra'Keisha again. She was doing a ninety-nine year bid. Ninety-nine or forty-nine, I'm riding until the wheels fall off.

I turned out the lights inside my motel room, peering around slowly before making an exit. I let out a deep breath as I came to the conclusion that today would be my last if I didn't come up with the funds some way, somehow.

After being denied yesterday at Mack City, I decided to give it another shot with a different club. I wore my other lingerie set underneath my sweatsuit. With just twenty-six dollars in my pocket, I headed towards Rhonda's house to meet Jaelyn.

Although my prison experience was horrible, the hundred dollars they gave me at the gate was a blessing. If keeping the motel wasn't enough stress, I pondered the idea of getting my state I.D. as well. My mother had been on my mind since the day I was escorted out of the nursing home. There was no way I'd be able to see her without proper identification.

I crossed the street towards the houses Rhonda resided in and strolled up the block. I hated the idea of asking her if I could sleep in her basement, but from the looks of things, that's where I was headed. I spotted Maine's car parked in the driveway and rolled my eyes. I knocked on the front door.

"Hey Syren," Rhonda greeted, pretending to be enthused by my presence.

"What's up, Rhonda? Where's Jaelyn?" I asked, peering past her.

"Jaelyn!"

Within seconds, Jaelyn arrived, papers in hand.

"Come on in, Syren," Rhonda voiced stepping to the side.

I walked inside and took a seat on the comfortable sofa. "Can I use a pen, Rhonda?"

"Sure. Hold on."

"Hold on, hold on. Jaelyn, I'll be back in a few hours. I have business to tend to," Maine said, walking past Jaelyn and me while holding the phone against his ear. His tank top was fitted and the Balmain shorts hung off his ass, exposing his briefs. His chain swung from side to side with each stride. This nigga was so motherfuckin' sexy. He caught me staring, then winked at me as he reached for the door.

"But Pop, I thought you were going to take me to get the new 12's," Jaelyn whined.

" I am, J. I'll take you tomorrow, I promise," he assured before walking out.

Jaelyn smacked his lips before reclining against the pillows on the sofa.

"You'll get them, Jaelyn. You know how your dad is."

"Yeah, I know. I wanted them today. Me and my friends suppose to wear them to Monty's house party later on tonight." He looked so upset, but there was nothing I could do.

"Come on, ride the bus with me to Foot Locker and I'll get them for you."

"For real, Ma? But how? Dad said that you were broke."

"Fuck what Maine told you. Let's go. Rhonda! We'll be back!"

~

Jaelyn and I entered the Foot Locker on Buckner. My palms instantly began to sweat. Luckily, the place was packed as if it was a tax-free weekend. I pretended to look as calm as possible.

"Come on, baby, show me the shoes," I spoke confidently.

I strolled behind Jaelyn. He spotted the black and white shoe instantly.

It's right there, Momma," he pointed.

I peered around the store, trying to spot the perfect candidate. "Bingo!" I mumbled, eyeing the dark-skinned brother who resembled Eddie Murphy when he starred in the movie *Norbit*. "Hey, excuse me, can I get a pair of those black and white twelve's in the size 7 please?" I requested, batting my lashes.

He loosened the top button on the collar of his shirt before saying, "Sure."

I strutted back over to Jaelyn and sat beside him on the bench. "I should be getting my own place soon. You going to come stay with me?"

"Sometimes, Momma," he replied dryly.

"I guess that's good enough."

"Here you go, ma'am," he said while handing me the shoebox.

"Try them on, son." I bent down with Jaelyn when he began to untie his shoes. "Put both of them on" I whispered. "I'll be back," I said, standing to my feet. "Can you go get me those pink and black Air Max right there?" I pointed as my left breast brushed his arm.

"Sure, give me one sec," he said before running off.

I quickly walked back towards Jaelyn. "Come on, baby," I said, trying not to appear rushed.

"You ready? I thought you were getting some too?"

"They don't have my size," I retorted, exiting the store. As soon as the air hit my cheeks, I deeply sighed in relief.

"Excuse me, ma'am, can you and your son step back inside?" an older white guy announced.

I looked at Jaelyn then back at him and nearly considered running, but I couldn't do it - not here and now with my son. I lowered my head and motioned Jaelyn back inside. All eyes were on us for a few seconds before people resumed what they were doing. We followed the white guy to the back.

"Sit down," he demanded. "Now usually I call the police and have you both fined and arrested, but I'm going to give you another chance. If you can call someone right now and they can pay for those sneakers on your feet, y'all both are free to go."

"You ain't said none but a word," Jaelyn responded, pulling out his phone. I knew he was calling Maine. This day couldn't get any worse. " Hey Dad, I know you said you're busy, but I'm up here at Foot Locker with mom about to go to jail if you don't come up here and pay for these stolen shoes she made me put on my feet."

My eyes bucked in shock. Although I was hurt and ashamed, it was the truth. I knew better than to pull a stunt like this. Jaelyn and I waited in the office in silence. I was hoping he'd say something, but he didn't.

"Hey, is this your dad?" The guy stood in the entryway of the office, pointing in the direction of someone in the store.

Jaelyn stood to see who he was pointing at. "Yes sir."

The guy motioned Maine over to the office.

"You dumb, dawg," Maine peered at me and said as soon as he entered. He tossed two crisp hundred dollar bills on the guy's desk and walked out. "I told you she was broke!" Maine yelled to Jaelyn as soon as they exited the store.

I lingered behind, there was no way I was going to ask Rhonda to sleep on her couch now. Jaelyn peered back at me before lowering his head.

"You out of line, Syren, for almost getting my boy locked up!" he yelled, staring at me in rage.

"He not even yours. He not even yours," I mouthed.

As soon as Maine read my lips he marched toward me. His eyes were twice their original size as he bit down on his bottom lip. "What you say, bitch? Huh, what you say?" He rushed me, peering at me devilishly with his fist balled by his side.

Alarmed, I continued to back away, but it didn't stop Maine from walking up on me.

"Bitch, I'll kill you if you ever say that shit out yo' mouth, broke ass," he mumbled. He mugged me before walking in the direction of his car.

Not wanting to give a dime to the city bus, I walked in the direction of the club. Soon I'd have to catch a bus since the other clubs were located along the highway. I felt so disgusted with myself I wanted to cry. I could've been on my way back to jail for some fucking Jordans. Let alone what my son just witnessed. What kind of parent was I?

I neared the Valero gas station. I decided to stop and grab something to put in my stomach to cease the growling. Making eye contact with no one in particular, I headed straight for the chip aisle.

"How you gon' put me on the back burner, Lisa? I told you I was on my way!" the guy screamed into the phone. I couldn't hear what the person on the other end was saying, but whatever it was, it didn't improve his mood. "You wrong, dawg. You know my baby has to be at her recital in a couple hours. I'm not about to send my kid up on stage with her hair looking like that."

I listened discreetly to his conversation while peering around for his daughter.

"You know what? Fuck you, bitch!" he yelled into the phone before ending the call.

I slid in line behind him with a pack of Flaming Hot Lays in my hand. I wanted to offer my services, but he was in such a rage I was afraid to bother him.

"Let me get $30 on pump two," he requested, tossing the bills on the counter. He turned to walk away before the cashier put the money into the register.

My palms were moist as hell, but it was now or never. Before he completely bypassed me, I grabbed him by his forearm. His head swiveled in my direction immediately. Once spotting me, his hard face softened, but not entirely.

"Excuse me, I wasn't being nosy or anything, but I overheard your conversation and if need be, I can do your daughter's hair. I'm a stylist myself."

"Okay, cool." He licked his lips and then grinned. "Where is your shop?"

"I don't have one."

"Well, where you stay?"

"Well, I'm waiting for my house to be built right now so I'm staying in a motel. I can do it at your place if it's cool. I don't bite," I added, flashing an innocent grin.

His brows were formed into a V as he stared at me skeptically. "Alright, ma, I can't be too picky. You're my only option right now."

"Let me pay for this real quick and I'm right behind you." I threw the chips and a five dollar bill on the counter, knowing damn well I had a single dollar and the exact change. I did otherwise so I wouldn't strike him as being broke. He waited for me and, after receiving my change, I followed him out.

"Hey ma, you have at least a half tank of gas? 'Cause I stay pretty far," he mentioned, peering over his shoulder at me.

I sighed before responding. "I don't have a car."

He stopped mid-stride, then eyed me head to toe. He opened his mouth to speak, yet nothing came out. He simply shook his head and proceeded towards his car. "Fuck it, I'm desperate."

***

Sir'Mahd

I peered up into the rearview mirror, discreetly eyeing the chick I had just picked up from the Valero gas station minutes ago. I'd seen her somewhere recently, but couldn't place it. Putting her in my ride and inviting her inside my crib, I was really testing my luck. Only two people knew about my residence in Irving. Her beauty aroused my senses, leaving me open and sincere. *A cute face gets a nigga every time*, I thought.

In spite of that, I was truly desperate. Amyah's piano recital was mere hours away and her hair was all over her head. I peered over at my baby girl, who sat on the passenger seat of my money green Range Rover. She bobbed her head to the Saweetie lyrics while peering out of the window.

My life had changed dramatically since Amyah's birth. I had gone from petty hustling to securing my own team of females and young hustlas working for me. As an adolescent, I watched my mother take someone's life and lose hers in the same setting. Unlike her victim, my mother lost her life to the system. At twenty-two years old, she was sentenced to eighty-five years. I didn't know the details until I was much older, but every day after that day, my grandmother would tell me my mom was returning soon. Every day when the rays from the sun woke me, I peered around the house and out the window through the fragile blinds in hopes of seeing my mother. The truth was revealed when my grandmother passed a few days after my fourteenth birthday from a massive heart attack.

Something in my gut told me to run, but I wasn't sure why. The police arrived and escorted me to this huge building. Inside, I remember a white lady asking me the same questions repeatedly. I didn't have anyone's contact information. It was just me and my grandmother. The white lady left me sitting there for what felt like hours before she returned.

A different lady returned, informing me that I would be placed into a foster home. I didn't know exactly what a foster home was, but I did know I'd be living under the same roof with a variety of kids who weren't related to me.

Enraged, I went on asking her questions and informing her about my mother's prompt appearance. The lady left only to return momentarily with information I wish she would have never fished for. Hearing that the earliest my mother could possibly return home was 2045 sent me crashing to the floor.

I remember awakening in an unfamiliar setting. I peered down at the bunk I lay in, instantly realizing it wasn't mine. Too afraid to get up, I calmed a bit once I spotted other kids sprawled out on bunk beds around me. I lay back on the hard cot and like a recap of a bad dream, I remembered the woman's words plain and clear once again. I felt like someone had stabbed me with a sharp knife. I gritted my teeth to prevent the screams from parting my lips as I cried like a starving newborn. I felt hopeless and helpless all at once. At that time I hated my grandmother for lying to me. I mourned the loss of my mother that night for the last night.

A few days later, I escaped from the foster home. Not a dollar in my pocket, living off hope. The first two nights I slept on the cold and unrelenting streets of Dallas. I hardly slept. I returned to the set of apartments I once stayed in with my mother, "The Oasis". Although the bench was slightly damp and cold, it was better than the pavement beneath my feet. After the second night, I still hadn't eaten. My stomach was touching my heart and the shit was hurting my feelings. I wanted to cry, but my pride outweighed the urge to grieve.

I needed food and a nice amount of rest, but I refused to return to the foster home. Later that evening I entered the Save A Lot grocery store. Praying no one spotted me on camera, I crept down the cereal aisle. I peered around to ensure no one was paying any attention to me, slid a couple of the boxes to the side, and lay on top of the metal shelf. I reached out and carefully placed the boxes in their original spot, shielding my body as well.

When I awoke from my slumber, it felt as if I'd been sleeping for days. The dimly-lit store told me it was closed. Afraid to set off any motion alarms, I quietly and slowly reached for the box of

Lucky Charms that blocked my torso, tore it open, and devoured them as if it was steak and potatoes.

I hung out on the block during the day and after the sunset, I crept my way back into the store. An older cat peeped my determination and availability and he took me under his wing. At fourteen, Dro introduced me to the drug game. The money was quick and easy.

A month or so later, I ended up meeting Amy. She stayed blocks from the area I hustled in. Across the street from the golf course was like the suburban part of OakCliff. She finessed and lied to her parents night after night to hang out with me. Her exclusive and unaccustomed appearance piqued my interest. The innocence behind her glistening emerald green eyes mesmerized me, but her willingness to conform to and respect my way of life only made me desire her even more.

Although times had changed, some things were still the same. Amy was white and so were both her parents, and later I found out that her dad was a racist. With the fast money I was making, every day was an adventure for Amy and me.

Then one day, that came to an end. I arrived in the hood after leaving the movies with Amy. I knew something had occurred after spotting the long faces and the huddle of people in large crowds. Immediately I was informed that Dro and two other dudes from around the way had been shot and killed. With the pack I had left, I got rid of it and cherished the profits instead of running through it like I had done previously. Before Dro's death I was sleeping in the clickhouse with him and a few others sometimes, but now I was back on the streets.

Knowing Amy would come like clockwork looking for me, I tried staying in pocket. In her presence, I had no worries or burdens. She captured my attention with no effort, extracting the soft and unguarded side of me. After hearing of my lack of shelter, she adamantly invited me to her home under certain circumstances. Unbeknownst to me, those circumstances were indeed strict. For two years I resided in Amy's cluttered but spacious walk-in closet.

Amy was a year older than me. As we awaited her eighteenth birthday, which was the approbation for her to move out, I had been hustling and saving as well. I used the money I profited off the packs of cocaine to purchase pills, Xans, and ecstasy pills. I would hang out at the corner store by the high school and sell to the high school kids and sometimes the men who occupied the barbershop beside the corner store. Amy even took a few to school to my customers who were unable to meet me at the store occasionally.

Up until her eighteenth birthday, Amy had snuck me food and water to eat and drink. I bathed when both her parents were away, which was hardly ever since they both had different work schedules. I pissed in many bottles, showered seldomly, and slept uncomfortably, afraid her father would find me asleep and pop my ass.

I had managed to save eight thousand dollars, not including the re-up money I had set aside for my next purchase. When it came time to finally move, I was happier than a sinner who was given the opportunity to ascend to heaven. I'd never been so ecstatic in my life. That night inside our apartment, sex had never been so amazing. During the first couple of steamy nights, we made Amyah.

As badly as she wanted to, I didn't allow Amy to work. I expanded my hustle, adding different merchandise, and that alone was more than enough to take care of my woman and seed. A year later, something life-changing and detrimental happened. Amy passed from breast cancer. They tried cutting the tumor out before it spread, but it was too late. It took her fast before we could suitably say goodbye.

Losing Amy was the second time I wept. I loved her as much as I loved the lady that birthed me. She gave me strength, loyalty, love, and assurance. Since Amy, I'd yet to date, feeling that no woman would ever amount to her. I kept my focus on my little angel and my money. Amyah had striking features: banana-colored skin, blonde curly hair, and those beautiful green eyes that had so enchanted me with her mother.

I grinded hard like I didn't have a dollar in my pocket. Slacking and sleeping was never an option. If I was going to get out of the game and be there a hundred percent for Amyah, I had to get the getting while the getting was good.

I couldn't help but sneak glances at the beauty who currently occupied my back seat. Most of the ride her eyes remain glued to the scenery outside her window. Something was heavy on her mind. She tried masking it with a smile every once in a while when she would look away and our eyes would meet, yet my ability to decipher the real from the fake just by analyzing someone's disposition made her appear naked through my transparent vision. Some things were hidden underneath the surface that even I couldn't pinpoint.

I parked in the driveway of my five bedroom home. I reached for my iPhone that rested in the cup holder, stealing one last glance at the chick in the backseat. I assumed she was lying about something she said earlier, yet her reaction to the setting around her was similar to someone who was accustomed to such surroundings. She simply curled her lips downward before climbing out of my truck.

"We're home, Ms. Lady," Amyah announced, running up the driveway, motioning the chick towards the porch. She wasn't selfish, snobby, and self- centered like most young girls. She was a daddy's girl to the fullest, yet she valued and enjoyed a woman's presence. Since her mother passed, my grandmother passed, and my mother was incarcerated, she was rarely graced with a woman's presence. I smiled at Amyah's elation while entering the massive house she and I shared.

I wasn't a millionaire - not even close to it - but if you Googled "hood rich", a picture of me would appear. I'd had trust issues since I was teen, therefore, I never considered a maid. Whether my bread was fast and illegal or slow and legal, I grinded too hard for my shit and I'd be damned if I gave anyone an accessible opportunity to take it from me.

"So baby girl, how is it that you want your hair?" she asked, finger combing through her curls.

"I want to look like a princess," Amyah requested.

"Can I holla at you real quick?" I asked, throwing my keys on the coffee table.

Stepping into my personal space, she said, "Yes."

"What's your name?"

"Syren."

"Syren, her hair products and stuff is in the cabinet inside her restroom. Let me know if you need anything else. I don't mind running you to the Walmart down the street."

She bit down on the corner of her bottom lip and I swear for that split second, my man throbbed. Her skin was flawless. Her bronze-colored skin glowed as if it was kissed by the sun.

"Let me check it out."

"No, Daddy, I'll show her," Amyah insisted, grabbing her by the hand and leading her down the long corridor.

I flopped down on the sofa. I was ready for this day to be over. Five minutes had passed, which was too long for me. I jumped to my feet to ensure "Syren" wasn't scoping for anything extra.

"Whew!" she sounded off as we nearly collided into each other. "I'm sorry, I didn't see you. What's your name?"

I hesitated before answering, not sure if I wanted to give her my name or my street name.

"Sir'Mahd."

"Sir'Mahd, we definitely need to take a trip."

***
<u>Syren</u>

A few items turned into a whole cart full of shit. This little girl was spoiled rotten. After grabbing the necessary items I'd need to transform Amyah into a little princess, I was ready to handle my business.

"Daddy, can I get this?" she asked, holding up the falsies. I peered back at Sir'Mahd in disbelief, my brows contorted into a V as I waited on his response.

"You not getting those, Amyah."

"Dad, but Ms. Syren has some," she whined.

"Ms. Syren grown. You'll have time to be grown, but for right now, you're a little princess. Ms. Syren is a Queen."

His words drew my next breath. Amyah peered up at me through her glistening green eyes. "Yes, sweetie, when you're a child you're a princess. As you age, you transform into a Queen."

She placed the falsies in the spot she got them from and said "Okay, Ms. Syren," flashing a huge grin.

We neared the register. I looked up at the clock on the wall. We had spent thirty-two minutes in this store.

"Ms. Syren, do you want my daddy to buy you something?"

"No, sweetie," I shot back. I could feel Sir'Mahd's eyes on me, which made me a bit jittery.

"Why, Ms. Syren? All of this is for me. The Queen deserves gifts too," she voiced with her hands clasped in front of her.

"I have all of this at home," I lied.

"Ooohh, Ms. Syren, you do? Can I come to your house and see all your Queen stuff?"

"Yes, one day you can," I replied nervously, placing the things on the counter.

~

"Sir'Mahd! I'm done!" I yelled. After arriving at his place, it took me less than thirty minutes to put li'l Miss Amyah on fleek. I pressed her coily hair out and trimmed her edges so that her wrap lay perfectly around her oval-shaped face. I applied one coat of mascara to her long lashes and painted her fingernails Barbie pink.

"Yeah," he dragged. His eyes grew once spotting Amyah. "She looks beautiful."

"Look at my nails, Dad," she blurted out.

"You ready?"

"Yes! I can't wait to play the piano with these," she responded, wiggling her fingertips.

"Go put your outfit on."

"Okay." She trotted off to her room and I began to clean things up.

"Hey, how much do I owe you?"

"Fifty."

He dug into his pocket, handing me what appeared to be more than fifty. I looked at him confused.

"That's for all your time, ma. I really appreciate you for helping me."

He possessed a solid and genuine aura. His pecan-colored skin complemented his camel-colored eyes. After every word or so, he'd run his thick tongue over his juicy pink lips. The thick scar that stretched diagonally across his chin didn't take from his handsomeness. It was simply a war wound, a reminder of his past that I wanted to know so much about. He had a gangsta and savage exterior, but on the inside, he wanted to love and be loved.

"Thank you, Sir'Mahd. I added all her new stuff to the top shelf," I said, heading for the door.

"Can I get your number? I'm going to fire Lisa's ass. She usually does Amyah's hair every two weeks."

I swallowed the lump in my throat. How do I tell a guy like him that I don't have a phone? "Well, Sir'Mahd, I got a dude, so just give me your number and a day prior, I'll call and we'll set something up."

His mouth curled downward as he handed me the phone. "Bet."

"Ms. Syren, are you coming to my recital?" Amyah yelled, running from the rear of the hallway.

"No, Amyah, but good luck and remember to have fun, sweetie."

" Okay, Ms. Syren, I will." She pouted.

"You sure you don't want me to give you a ride to your motel?" he asked, rubbing the bottom of his chin.

"Yes, I'm sure," I responded.

Our eyes lingered for seconds too long. I tried remaining cool and unperturbed, but his piercing brown eyes made me feel shy and skittish like a teenage girl again. I said my goodbyes and dashed out of the house and down the porch.

***

Roses, I walked in the corner
with the body screaming dolo.
Never sold a bag, but look like Pablo in the photo.
This gon' make 'em feel
The way like Tony killed Manolo
You already know though, you already know though.
I walk in the corner with the money on my finger.
She might get it poppin',
I might wife her for the winter.
I already know, already know, nigga, roses.
All I need is roses."

I used the money Sir'Mahd blessed me with to buy a pair of six-inch, bedazzled platform heels and an exotic two-piece. I re-touched my goddess braids and flawlessly applied my makeup. The shimmery eye shadow and beat face looked immaculate, enhancing my natural beauty. I bopped through the club like I owned it. Ass on fat, stomach on flat. You couldn't tell me shit. The owner just saw a glimpse of my round apple bottom and I was in.

Although the night was young, my confidence was deteriorating by the minute. The poorly put together club was more ratchet than it appeared. Dudes wasn't trying to pay for a dance. They were throwing money so they could lay up in something. The sight of it all disgusted me. Two hours had passed and all I had managed to make was a hundred measly bucks.

"Say, li'l momma."

I didn't even bother to acknowledge him.

"Say, let me holla at you."

I exhaled deeply before turning on my heels. "What's up?" I asked, trying not to appear irritated.

"I got three hundred dollars if you got that W.A.P."

I smacked my lips and then strutted off. If I was going to make some bread dancing, I was going to have to blow this joint and make my way to an upscale club.

"So you're too good for V.I.P?" the light-skinned chick who stood posted up against the dressing room asked.

"I'm trying to pop pussy, not pass any out," I retorted, eyeing the three chicks who peered at me in resentment.

"Oh, well this the land of the savages. It's a reason why certain dudes come here. 'Cause they know anything goes. If you not down for the green light special, you might need to test your luck up the street."

"You right. I don't want no smoke. Excuse me," I said, bypassing them and retrieving my things out of the locker. I got my little hundred dollars and walked off like a model.

"Hey."

I turned around and peered into the eyes of the dude with the raspy voice.

"You trying to make some real bread?"

"I'm not selling no pussy."

"You don't have to do that. I don't buy that shit anyways. You might have to show it though."

"I don't mind doing that. It's part of my profession."

"Follow me to the lot. I'm going to give you the rundown."

I was quite hesitant, but my needs outweighed it all. I was tired of being treated like the help.

***

Maine

I sat across from Cocoa at the oddly-shaped table inside the Chinese restaurant that was located in the rear of North Park Mall. After a couple of phone calls and a galore of texts, she decided to meet me here. Never in my life have I wanted something so bad, but I was about ready to take sum' if she held out any longer.

"So, you got any kids? I asked, pretending to care.

"No, do you? I would like two, maybe a boy and a girl, or two boys."

"That's cool. I got a little man. He'll be fifteen in a few months."

"You thinking about giving him a tour of the club for his birthday?" she asked before winking.

"If that's what he wants, but he's really not into girls. All he cares about is sports and school." No sooner had the words left my lips than I spotted Uh'Nija's little cousin Bianca.

"Heeey Maine!" she yelled, waving her hand, signaling for me to come over.

I remained calm, but the last thing I wanted her to do was tell Uh'Nija. I'd never hear the end of it.

"What's up, Bianca?"

The corner of her lip was raised as her nostrils spread. "Who is that? And where is my cousin?"

"That's just a friend, man."

"Do my cousin know about your friend?" she asked, putting emphasis on the word friend.

I loathed whenever she placed her hand on her hip as if she was grown. " Just do me a favor and don't say anything to your crazy-ass cousin."

" Okay, well do me a favor and loan me two hundred dollars."

I reached in my pocket to retrieve the cash. "You mean give you two hundred dollars? You know you not going to pay me back."

She snatched the money and vanished around the corner.

"Why you looking at your watch?" I asked Cocoa, coming up from behind.

"Boy, you scared me." She placed her hand over her chest.

"Come on, let's do a little shopping."

Cocoa and I conversed freely while browsing around a few stores. The pink Balenciagas had her whispering sweet nothings in my ear since the moment I bought them. I listened attentively to Cocoa as she rambled about her past. I spotted and quickly veered inside the Chanel store. I knew the feminine and expensive boutique would seal the deal.

"What's up, Maine?" Zula greeted me as soon as I neared the counter. He and I had gotten close due to the numerous visits.

"'Sup, Z, what you got new?" I asked, peering around aimlessly.

Zula looked up at me, flashing a sinister smile. "I got this in this morning," he said, holding up the gold chunky chain Chanel necklace.

"You like that?" I pointed while eyeing a stunned Cocoa.

"I love it!" she yelped, wrapping her arms around my neck.

"How much, Z?"

"Fourteen fifty."

I reached into my pocket and counted it out, then handed him the money. My phone rang in the process. I motioned for Cocoa to give me a second as I jogged to the entryway of the store. It was Uh'Nija.

"Hello?"

"Don't whisper, nigga!" she yelled. She sounded louder than someone speaking into the other end of the receiver. "So this what you doing now?" She appeared in front of me, enraged. By that time, she had obtained the attention of both Zula and Cocoa.

I sighed heavily while rolling my eyes. I could slap fire from Bianca's young ass. "Calm down——"

"Don't tell me shit! I hate you!" she yelled.

I could feel her distress. I'd seen the same look in Syren's eye time and time again. She hated how much she loved me, yet she lacked the strength to walk away. She cursed herself for falling for a guy like myself. I can't say her tears didn't move me. Surely, they did. However, not enough for me to forget about the piece of pussy standing behind me.

"What's happening, Maine?" Cocoa walked up, appearing dumbfounded.

"Just fall back. Let me handle this."

"Nah, let's hear what your bitch has to say!"

"Bitch?" Cocoa shot back.

"Yeah, you heard – wait." Uh'Nija peered closely down at the shopping bag. She turned her nose up at me while eyeing me through narrow slits before blurting, "You bought this bitch some Balency's?"

I didn't even get a chance to respond before Uh'Nija pounced on me, scarring my face with her claw-like nails. I wrapped my arms around her tightly to cease the attack as I squeezed my eyes shut to avoid getting poked in the eye. The open wounds had already begun to burn. When I did slightly open my eyes, I noticed all the people that surrounded us with their phones out.

It was pathetic that they'd rather go viral than attempt to render aid. I could hear Uh'Nija's squeaky-ass voice, however, her blows seem to have ceased. I peered up confusedly at a rage-filled and wildly swinging Uh'Nija. At some point, she and Cocoa had gotten entangled. I removed my arms from around her waist and planted her ten toes on the pavement.

Although Cocoa was taller and thicker, Uh'Nija was beating her like a drum. Uh'Nija was indeed hurting - and not in a physical sense. Groans escaped her mouth through clenched teeth as she swung militantly. I forced myself in between the two, enduring a few blows myself before they finally decided to stop.

"Uh'Nija, go home. I'm on my way," I voiced, peering into her exhausted eyes.

Her chest heaved as she tried to regain control of her breathing. The only thing she was tired of was dealing with me. "Nah, stay right here where you at. I'm done! On God," she swore before walking away in the opposite direction.

Uh'Nija had threatened to leave many times before, but something about today bore more conviction.

"You got your necklace?" I asked Cocoa while helping her pick up the shopping bags that were placed neatly in front of the boutique.

"Yeah," she replied in a low tone.

"You mad at me?" I asked, peering up ahead at the exit.

"Nah. Now I'm curious to know what is it that got her risking her freedom coming way out here to fight me in the middle of the mall," she said, shooting me a sexy wink. She traced her thick lips with the tip of her tongue and at that moment, I forgot about Uh'Nija and what had just taken place. I flashed Cocoa a smile as we neared the exit door. I peered around to make sure there wasn't any sign of Uh'Nija while strolling towards my car.

Suprisingly, it wasn't keyed, nor were the tires flat or the windshield busted. *Hopefully she didn't put anything in my gas tank*, I thought while inspecting it thoroughly.

Minutes later, Cocoa's warm, wet mouth covered my penis. Since it was difficult to concentrate, I drove ten miles under the speed limit.

"Fuck that bitch, Maine," she whispered, peering up into my eyes. Saliva lubricated and dripped slowly from her lips as she teased me, circling her tongue inside and around my pee hole.

"Quit playing with me," I said, slowly thrusting my hips.

Like a chick that hadn't eaten in days, she feasted on my mans as if it had a pair of legs to flee. Sweat beads formed across my head as I tried holding back, clenching my teeth and booty cheeks to impede the inevitable release. I just wanted to enjoy the satisfaction and warmth of her mouth for a few more minutes.

"Aaarrghh!" I roared like I was auditioning for a role in *The Lion King*. I was so certain she wouldn't survive the impact of the forceful gust of semen that barged its way through and down her throat.

She locked both hands around my penis, squeezing it tightly while swallowing everything that flowed from it. She double tapped it against her tongue to ensure there was nothing left and licked the tip clean before scooting over to her side.

Although I'd never admit it, that was the best throat I ever had in my life.

***

Sir'Mahd

Shorty had been on my mind since she flew out of my crib. When she wasn't there, Amyah constantly reminded me. Something about Syren's spirit meshed well with both Amyah's and mine.

I veered onto Stovall Drive and parked a few houses down from my spot. Lowkey, I had been hoping we'd cross paths again.

"I'm outside."

"Bet," King replied before hanging up.

I had met King at East Field College while studying for an Associate's Degree in Business Management. I thought I'd be able to juggle school and the streets, but I was wrong. Money came, and the drama wasn't too far from it. I didn't trust anyone to take care of Amyah, so I dropped out. Later, King did too. We vibed effortlessly. He was wise beyond his years and always possessed a positive aura. After taking a chance on him, I admired his grind. It actually reminded me of my own, and that's why I considered him my right hand man. Because of King, I didn't have to get my hands dirty unless I chose to. He was proven.

"What's up, boy?" I asked, entering his place. His place could use renovation to a certain degree. Years of being in the game and he never even considered purchasing a place with more seclusion. I just hoped he would never regret it.

"Man, I wanted you to meet me here because I need to holla at you about something."

Instinctively, I frowned as my heart began to race. The last thing I wanted to be in the pen sharing showers. "Shoot," I replied, appearing calm.

"Someone stealing."

I discreetly sighed a breath of relief. "Stealing?"

"Yeah, fam, and my gut telling me it's the hoes and not them young dudes. I could be wrong, Mahd, but I just think I'm right," he stated seriously, peering at me through burdened eyes.

"How long you think it's been occurring?"

"I can't call it exactly, but I can tell you it's not the first time."

"Well, if they are stealing, they must be stuffing that shit pretty deep. They still bend over and spread, right?"

"The routine is still the same."

"Come on, I haven't been over in a minute. After I get done spectating, we'll plot from there."

King and I left his place and headed to the spot. Instead of merely walking a few houses down and entering, we took the route that led to the rear of the place. A light fog pervaded the small but suitable house. I peered around the empty living room.

"Where Terry and them at?" I asked.

"They posted up at the car wash. You know it's rush hour."

"You sure is right," I agreed, making my way towards the kitchen. I moved the sheet that was posed as a curtain to the side as I entered the kitchen, instantly, spotting three women. Two of the ladies possessed bodies that resembled masterpieces.

"Damn, Tonya, what happened?" I asked while peering at her saggy breasts and pot belly in disgust. Tonya was the only one of the three I was familiar with. Hiring the women was my idea, but I didn't keep track of the ones who were employed. Tonya was someone I referred years ago. We hustled on the same block at one point, but she vanished one day. I later found out she was locked up for failing to render aid while a murder had taken place, and when she returned home, she wanted to hustle again. However, I didn't trust nor did I know her well enough to add her to my team, so I propositioned her to be one of the few women to cook, cut, and weigh the dope.

King chuckled pitilessly. He laughed so hard I began to laugh as well when in reality, I was truly curious.

"Fuck you, King! Mahd, I had a baby a few months ago and I can't seem to snap back. Buy a bitch a body," she suggested with her hand on her hip.

"You make enough to buy your own body!" I shot back. I discreetly examined the other ladies, who were awfully quiet.

"You still the same. You still single?" she pried.

"You still trying to find out?" I retorted before signaling King back to the front. I left Tonya standing there looking dumbfounded. King and I needed to talk somewhere private.

"Hey, isn't it four? Where's the other one?" I asked curiously.

"She always a little late. She's having car complications, so she rides the bus. I hired her two days ago."

"More than likely it's Tonya. She's been here a long time. She's comfortable. She knows too much, certainly the ins and outs. Comfort will get you every single time. Doing it all this time she has gotten sloppy, but it's no telling how long she been hittin' our asses."

"You want me to get rid of her?"

"Nah, 'cause it's a slim chance I could be wrong. Then again, we can't sleep on the new chick. I'ma stick around so I can feel her out."

"You right."

"For now, we adding cameras to the restroom. Give they asses zero privacy. Something will surface soon." I tried waiting for the new chick as King and I discussed a new few business ideas, but the way my schedule was set up, I couldn't wait any longer. Amyah got out of school in less than thirty minutes.

"Alright, boy," King said as I stood to my feet.

"Stay alert. Hit me up if something comes up," I voiced, peering back at him before walking out the door.

I hopped inside my Impala SS before pulling off. Only once a week I'd splurge around in the classic. As I neared the stop sign, I peered through my rearview at the city bus passing by. Shorty was digging in her purse as she made her way down the street. It might not be today, tomorrow, or even next week, but soon I'd be seeing about her as well.

***

Syren

"Damn, that Impala nice," I voiced barely over a whisper as I admired the classic green car accelerating past the stop sign. The paint job was the color of green grass with a slight coating of dew that sparkled flawlessly from the beam of sunlight. I didn't tell King, but prior to arriving I had visited the DMV to get my license. I needed to see my mother as much as I needed to take my next breath. Although I didn't possess much, you couldn't tell. Yesterday after leaving "work", I purchased a few bags of braid hair and styled my hair into box braids. The braids were neat, medium-sized, and hung right above the crack of my ass. I bought underclothes, a nice pair of sandals, and three outfits from the clearance rack inside Nordstrom's, so things were progressing for me. Oh, and I purchased a phone. The iPhone 8. I wasn't approved for a newer version.

"Hey King," I spoke upon entering.

"What's up?" he answered, eyeing me from head to toe.

I couldn't decipher if he wanted to speak on my tardiness or my appearance. Whatever it was, I assumed he reconsidered since he closed the door behind me and flopped down on the sofa.

I proceeded to the rear of the house, bypassing the other three women. I spotted Tonya nudge Neko with her elbow. I kept walking without speaking on the matter.

"Hey girl," Tonya greeted, pretending to be enthused.

I saw right through her ass. Her bad built ass didn't deserve to work here no ways. "What's up?" I asked as I turned to face her.

"Shit, we been waiting on you," she responded.

"Oh, okay, I'll be back." Something about Tonya's vibe I just couldn't fall in with. She had a motive and I was going to sit back and wait until it emerged.

While on duty, we were allowed to wear sheer undergarments if we didn't want to be nude. Since I've been low on funds, I reconsidered purchasing the material when I had other options. Besides, Neko, Meka, and Tonya were nude, so I didn't feel out of place. However, even as an adolescent, I preferred to do things differently. I've always set my own trends and had my own swag. The pink sheer bra and thong made a bitch look edible, like a strawberry shortcake. I did a 360 in the full-length mirror. It didn't matter if my workplace was suitable or appropriate. As a woman, I must represent myself.

Since meeting Sir'Mahd, he had managed to invade my thoughts more than I'd like him to. Occasionally I envisioned a life with him in it. He made me feel worthy and royal, yet sheepish and sensitive at the same time. I feared no man but God. The demanding and stoic aura I felt whenever I was in his presence made me a bit uneasy, but in a good way.

The girls stared at me as I entered the kitchen. Envy oozed from their pores, and I saw their noses wrinkle and the corners of their lips curl upwards. I knew they were hatin'. I was going to have to keep a keen eye on all of these bitches because Envy was indeed the worst of them all. There's no limit to the amount of damage an envious bitch can cause.

I went to retrieve the work from King and took my place beside Neko. I bobbed my head to the trap music that played at a low tone.

"You look so sexy, Syren," Meka complimented through squinted eyes.

I chuckled at her bold comment then said, "Thank you, girl!"

"Are you going to King's birthday party next weekend?"

"Birthday party?" I inquired inquisitively.

"Well, it's supposed to be a surprise party," she admitted, leaning in closer.

"Well, I d——"

"Now you know that at least one of us has to be here to pick up the slack," Tonya intervened.

"Yeah, and I thought we decided it was going to be you, Tonya," Meka shot back.

"Yeah, it was, but I changed my mind. Besides, King and his people don't even know her like that."

"What difference does that make? Niggas love bad bitches."

"I know that, and that's why I decided to go. She can catch the next one," she said before winking.

"Look, 'preciate ya, Meka, but I need the bread anyways. Clubbing isn't on my agenda right now," I stated, cutting my eyes at Tonya's ratchet ass. If she thought for a second that she had anything on me, she was delusional. That bitch better buy her a body before she'd be any competition. The only thing that was cute was her golden-brown complexion and her big round eyes. Her lips looked like Kylie Jenner's before the injections and her nose was wide as hell. However, I don't blame her for wishful thinking. If you don't believe in yourself, no one else will.

"Okay, cool. I would come fuck with ya, but King is my boy. Plus I'm trying to catch Sir's fine ass."

"You good. Go turn up. Who is Sir?"

"The H.N.I.C. He comes by seldomly. I try to keep things professional, but Saturday I'm gon' try to give it all that I got. You hear me?" I could hear Tonya smack her lips in the background.

"She got a thing for Sir too, but he pays her no mind," Meka whispered. Meka was dark-skinned and bowlegged. Her dark skin was smooth and soft, free of any blemishes. Her teeth were beautiful and white with a gold tooth on each side. Her body was proportioned precisely. Bitches prayed and paid for a body like that. She seemed ratchet, but that wasn't a problem for most dudes these days. Megan Thee Stallion had really paved the way for ratchets.

"Hey, maybe you'll make a little extra, being that you'll be the only one here."

"Hopefully, 'cause I sure can use it."

We were paid a hundred and fifty bucks a day to turn a kilo of soft into hard, then bust it down into fifty, dub, and dime packs. Whenever we finished the key, we were free to go, which usually took between three and a half to five hours. It always took Tonya three and a half hours, perhaps four if she was pussy-footing around. Meka and Necko would finish ten to fifteen minutes after her. I was a bit rusty. The last time I had cooked and bagged dope was my teenage years after Maine and I had first gotten acquainted. In a month's time I'd be four thousand dollars richer, and that meant everything to me. For now, the motel and city bus would have to do it. A part of me despised missing the party to work. The quickest come-up is a balling ass nigga. However, Tonya was right about one thing. I'd make the next one, and best believe I was going to shut shit down.

Since I arrived so late. I knew it's going to be a long day. I hadn't seen or heard from Jaelyn since the Foot Locker incident. Cognizant of the fact that I could only do so much since I had nothing to offer, I figured I'd just get some sort of stability before bothering him again.

Tonya had rushed out minutes ago, claiming she had someplace to be, but we all knew that was a lie and she really felt some kind of way. She needed to consider glueing her lace wig down at the back if she knew she hadn't had a perm in years.

Before long, I stood in the kitchen alone, doing my thing. I listened to Hot Tracks on spotify from my phone while doing so. King checked on me a few times, trying to make conversation, but I kept it short. Yesterday I would've entertained him and been flattered by the attention from him, but after learning about the mysterious Sir, I was more than intrigued. I was interested in finding about more and possibly making him mine.

***

I took a deep breath once my feet hit the pavement after exiting the bus. The last time I'd been to the nursing home, I almost got arrested. Seeing the woman that birthed me in such a traumatic state sent me over the edge.

"Give me strength, Lord," I prayed in a low tone.

Entering the nursing home, I spotted the security guard and he didn't recognize me. I mugged him and proceeded to the front desk. Before I said anything, I placed the paper I.D. on the counter.

"I'm here to visit Sheila Minks."

"You're her——"

"Daughter," I chimed in. Honestly, I was still upset with her hating ass since the last incident.

She called the room number and pointed. "Use that elevator down the hall to your left."

I snatched my I.D. from her hand and made my way down the hall. She seemed appalled by my attitude, but I didn't give a damn. I stepped off the elevator and suddenly my pace slowed. Fear slowly seeped through my body as I made my way down the hallway. I stopped in front of the door, gathering my thoughts before entering. I slowly opened the door, stepping inside. Seeing my mother alone truly bothered me.

"Hey Momma," I voiced weakly.

"Hey baby, you made it home!" she yelled, certainly enthused as her eyes bucked in excitement. She wrapped her arms around my neck, startling me. I was confused.

"Momma, I——"

"Baby, take me home with you. You know I'm not used to this. I'm too grown for a bedtime," she intervened as she continued her ramble.

"I'm living in a motel right now, Momma, but that's about to change real soon. I got a good job."

"When did you get home, Syren?" she asked as the wrinkles formed across her forehead.

"About two weeks ago. I came up here to see you, but you acted like you didn't know me," I confessed, peering into her eyes. Something was different about my mother, which I found very disquieting, yet there was nothing I could do but go forward from here. I didn't want to ask any questions that'd force her into the insane state she was in my last visit. *Maybe she really didn't see me?* I thought. But I was only fooling myself. I had looked my mother dead in her eyes, and she returned the stare then looked past me. I didn't care how she got here. All I knew is that she'd be out of here soon. She bathed me, clothed me, fed me, and changed my pissy and shitty diapers. The least I could do is return the favor. I fetched snacks and drinks from the vending machine and enjoyed my mother's company for the next two hours.

I was heartbroken when the lady informed me that my time was up. I knew my mother wasn't in her right head when she happily hugged and kissed me on the cheek while saying goodbye. I held onto her for dear life.

"I'll be back to get you," I whispered, letting her go. I eyed her until I was standing outside her door and in the hallway. I spoke with the front desk clerk in regards to proper steps that'd be necessary for me to bring my mother home.

The grind just got real, I thought, stepping foot out of the nursing home.

~

"Hey, Wiley!" Mr. Jimmy called out.

He was an older guy who ran the front desk in the small office near the entrance of the motel.

"Yes?" I backpedalled, wondering what the hell he could possibly want.

"You have mail," he said, holding it in his hand.

I forgot I had written Symphony and RaKeisha using the motel address. Surprisingly, we were able to receive mail at this piece of shit.

"Thank you," I said, retrieving it and walking out.

RaKeisha hadn't responded right away, but Symphony did. I slid inside my motel room and opened Symphony's letter.

Syren,

You were one of the realest bitches I ever met in this hell hole and when I get out, I'm going to be looking for that ass with a flashlight. I don't have long at all, so don't be surprised when I pull up on you.

Symph.

I smiled while reading the letter. Her ass always managed to lift my spirits, and that's what I adored about her the most. I tossed the letter and envelope on the table and turned on the shower so I could head to the spot.

One week later
Maine

"Jaelyn?" I hollered.

"Huh?" he called out.

"Have you talked to your mother?"

"No sir."

"Alright."

Jaelyn scurried back to his room. Syren had been on my mind since I spoke those venomous words to her. I couldn't fathom why I felt so remorseful. I thought about her living arrangement and wondered if she was maintaining. Hopefully she was. Since I'd known Syren, she possessed ambition. When I first met her, I learned that she was making money sewing for the other chicks in her apartment complex. The alterations didn't make her much money, but it was something and it was hers. Syren was more than my fiancée at the time when we were a couple. She was family. I missed her cheerful spirit. She was always so energetic and adventurous, there to pick up my slack and clean up my fuck-ups. I truly wanted her to be a part of my life, but I don't think I'd ever have the courage or be able to set aside my pride and admit it.

"You have reached th——"

Since the mall incident, I had tried phoning Uh'Nija every day, but after the first ring, the automated service interrupted. Today was different. I was adamant about reaching her. After visiting her place yesterday to find it vacant, I'd become a bit disturbed. She even deleted and blocked me from her Twitter and Instagram. She was a sucka for social media ,so I doubt if she deleted her accounts.

I had been spending more time with Cocoa since Uh'Nija was no longer in the equation. Although our sex life was breathtaking and refreshing, I didn't want to commit to anything. Syren left me emotionally scarred, and even though Uh'Nija deserved her karma, I left her dismantled and desolated. I was tired of going through the motions with the women in my life.

"Aye Dad?" Jaelyn called out, appearing in the doorway.

"What's up?"

"Can I use your card later to order the fight?"

"Yeah, here, just preorder it right now. I'll be at the club later."

He grabbed the card and vanished. I made a mental note to watch the fight whenever I was done at the club. Halloween weekend at Mack City. It was going down.

***

Like Club God said, throw that ass, poke it out
I ain't gay, but I let a bitch eat me out (Yeah)
Bad bitch and my bitches too.

Take all these niggas' money what we finna to do
Then leave, then leave get that bread, get that
Head then leave

I bopped through the club like Diddy, pleased to see everyone having a good time. The costumes were charming and sexy. Nothing you'd wear to go trick or treating, unless sex was the treat and the men were tricking. There were bunnies, devils, hoes, pimps, actresses, witches, and fairies. They all had one thing in common. They were drippin' with sex appeal.

Cocoa, Candy Redd, and P. Mula entered the packed club dressed like hoes with the exception of Cocoa appearing to be the pimp. I just knew she was going to come half-naked trying to shut shit down to obtain some sort of emotional reaction from me, but surprisingly, she didn't. She wore a red Prada frock coat and matching bell-bottom hip-huggers. The shirt she wore underneath was unbuttoned, easily revealing the rose gold Tiffany and Co. chain with beveled links. The Givenchy hip bag and 18K white gold diamond ring really complemented the look. The low ponytail brought her comely features to light. She peered at me unblinkingly, matching my gaze as she used her tongue to twirl and flip the toothpick in her mouth.

"Y'all ladies looking good," I complimented, eyeing them all through desirous eyes. Fantasizing about the tight nectar between their legs made the organ between my thighs buck in excitement.

"Thank you," they all spoke in unison.

"Hey, didn't I tell you hoes to keep your heads down?" Cocoa snapped.

I chuckled at her attempt to imitate such a masculine and ruthless role.

Candy Redd peered up at me out the corner of her eye. Images of her tiny pretty pink snatch flashed vividly through my mental.

"We'll catch up later," Cocoa voiced, jolting me from my thoughts.

Candy Redd winked as she strutted off. I simply shook my head in agreement at Cocoa's statement. After watching Candy Redd walk away, it left me speechless for a moment. I couldn't shake the young tender from my mind. I stood a few feet from the entryway, greeting everyone who showed up to another one of my events.

"We ten people over the capacity, Bossman."

"Huh?" I asked, regaining consciousness. "My bad, man, what you say?" I continued.

"We ten people over the capacity."

"About how many is it waiting outside in the line?"

"Twenty, give or take."

I peered around while thinking of a solution. I hated to leave my customers disappointed.

"Hold up!" I shouted over my shoulder to Jerry after spotting the empty table. "Hey, you mind helping me move this to the back?" I asked a dude who happened to be standing beside the table.

"Yeah, come on," he responded, handing his drink to the lady that stood beside him.

Although the club was jam-packed, we had no problem making our way to the back with not just a table, but a few chairs as well.

"We good, Jerry," I assured him, standing on the side of him, watching the rest of the crowd fall in. "Once they're inside, close the door," I ordered through clenched teeth while smiling and shaking a few hands.

Once the door was closed, I wandered around the club. My mind appeared to move about aimlessly too as the thought of losing Uh'Nija surfaced. Halloween was her favorite holiday. Each year she never ceased to amaze me with the weird and sexy costumes she wore - attire I would despise and ban her from wearing in public because it caused too much unwanted attention, but I loved to see her in it within the privacy of one another. I diverted my attention to my phone that vibrated continuously in my pocket.

"Come see me for once. C.Redd." The text from the unknown number confused me for a split second but after seeing the "C.Redd", I instantly knew what time it was.

"Where you at?" I replied back quickly while peering around for Cocoa. I was going to at least attempt to be discreet about linking up with her sister. I knew Candy Redd was somewhere waiting on me cause she damn sure wasn't with Cocoa and P. Mula, who sat in the V.I.P. tossing shots of Henny back.

"Hey, I want you to get dressed and get on stage," I snapped, invading Cocoa's personal space.

"Huh?" she asked, appearing dumbfounded by my sudden request.

"A few guys have made personal requests for you and I want to see you turn this bitch out," I lied, trying to sound convincing as possible.

"That's cool, but I thought you told me the other night you didn't want me shaking my ass half-naked in the clubs no more and you wanted me all to yourself?" she replied woefully. Her cheerful and upbeat mood had vanished as soon as the words left my mouth. She looked exhausted. Her nose flared. She was obviously angry, yet her eyes were indistinct. It was the same glare Uh'Nija and Syren had given me. "Come on, P," she voiced, rolling her eyes at me."

"Where you at?" I resent the text a second time while ensuring P.Mula and Cocoa headed to the dressing room. I watched from a distance.

"The office."

I shot out like I had fire underneath my feet.

"Aye Jerry, I'm about to disappear for about twenty, thirty minutes. I'll be in the office, but if you need me, hit my jack."

"Alright, bet."

I slowly twisted the knob on the door before opening it, immediately spotting Candy Redd bent over on all fours on top of the round table. My mouth watered as I quickly slid in and closed and locked the door behind me. Nothing but a thong and bra covered her skin, which was the color of honey and creamy butter. I undressed slowly while watching her unblinkingly.

"How you want it, daddy?" she asked, tracing her lips with her tongue.

"Get back in that position you were in. Instead of you putting those hands on the table, reach around and grab your ankles," I requested, smirking mischievously. I wanted to see how flexible this chick was.

Effortlessly, she completed the task within seconds. My mans stretched the material of my boxers as it rose instantly. I yanked them down to my ankles. I watched her eyes buck in excitement as she gazed down at my sizable penis. Using her teeth, she clamped down on the corner of her bottom lip, eyeing me lustfully as I stroked myself slowly. I smiled as I peered up at her, waiting to hear her beg for it. She slowly slid her thong down her smooth long legs without breaking our gaze. I sped up the pace as I thought of a hundred different positions I could use and abuse her in.

"Cum for me, daddy," she spoke in a low and seductive tone.

Everything she did and said aroused me to the highest degree. My bottom lip quivered as my breathing became shallow.

"Where you want it?" I mouthed.

She peered up at me deviously and patted the top of her perfectly-shaved kitten.

"Mmmmmm!" I clenched my teeth as I used the table for support. My legs became weak, then a warm, thick, creamy liquid gushed out like a water hose. I had every intention to put it where she wanted it to go, but once I saw the liquid flow down her wig and past her brows I reconsidered. She opened her mouth wide and I took aim. She caught it down to the last drop. She used the tip of her index finger to swipe away the mess I made up top that now lay directly in the crease of her eyelids, which sort of blended in with the white, pearl tint creamy eyeshadow. She swiped a few times then sucked her finger clean.

"Get it back hard," I requested, lowkey impatient. I was ready to get a felt of that WAP. She hopped down off the table, stepping into my personal space. In a swift motion, she dropped low into a squat, using her soft and freshly manicured hands to massage my mans.

"Use ya hand to choke that motherfucka, then wrap ya lips around it," I blurted, feeling impatient.

She did exactly as I instructed like she had been given permission. It took no time to stiffen up, and as soon as it did, we sexed like it was the last time. Her little pussy hugged my dick perfectly, like it was specifically made for me. Her box was so tight it made it difficult to dig in and around.   When we switched positions and she got on top, I felt so powerless and defenseless, exposed. I hated to feel that way, but the grunts and faces plus the inability to hold on revealed just how superbly the young tender was putting it down.

We both came a number of times, nearly clearing a whole box of condoms. We got dressed to leave, but before she reached for the knob, I reached for her hand, ceasing her movement.

"Hey, when am I going to see you again?"

"You tell me," she responded in a low, hushed tone.

"I guess whenever you're free and feeling a nigga."

"No, you the man with all the plans. What about Cocoa?"

"What about her? We not together. I'm trying to see about me and you," I admitted stepping closer. Her breath smelled like sex and candy, which was subtle compared to the musky smell.

"We'll see. You have my number," she said before walking out.

I walked out seconds behind Candy Redd only to be met by Cocoa's gaze merely a short distance away. Her arms were crossed at her chest as she stared at me with pure hatred in her eyes. I cursed myself underneath my breath for being so careless and reckless. If looks could kill, I'd be on a gurney with a white sheet placed over me. She shook her head from side to side, frowning in disgust.

"You's a fuck boy!" she shouted over the loud music.

"Cuz I didn't give you any of this good dick? Hold what you got. It's enough to go around," I shot back with a huge grin.

"We'll see how long you'll be smiling," she voiced, walking away.

"Cocoa! Wait, come here!"

She stopped, then turned around to listen.

"Look, man, just chill. I was just gassin'. Nothing happened. I wouldn't do you like that," I attempted to convince her, hoping she'd get with it, but if not, I didn't give a fuck either way. I hated that I was so reckless. I figured if I made Cocoa work tonight, she'd be too occupied to keep up with me, but like I've done before. I

74

allowed time to slip away. She was already dressed and waiting on my ass.

***

<u>Syren</u>

The bus ride from the spot to the motel was pretty lengthy, but I tried my best not to complain. I'd been busting my ass every day to change the poor living arrangement. Sir'Mahd was still heavy on my mind and when the time came for me to contact him about Amyah's touch-up, I realized my irresponsible ass misplaced the number. I kept hoping I'd find it Each night after work I'd scan around for it.

I sped up my pace as I practically jogged through the dark and deserted parking lot. I retrieved the key from my purse, unlocking the door.

Aaagghhh!" I shrieked in horror upon feeling the hand on my shoulder. I turned my head, instantly spotting Symphony. A sigh of relief escaped my lips as I placed my hand over my heart.

"Your scary ass gon' fuck around and kill yourself," Symphony joked.

"Shut the hell up and get in here," I voiced, walking inside.

It had been a little over a month since I last seen her and surprisingly, nothing had changed. She did look different in the oversized clothes in spite of the imperfections she used to gripe about. The one size big T-shirt complimented her swag and hid the small fat roll she'd accumulated around the abdominal area as well as her voluptuous ass. I used to tell Symphony continuously to slow down on the burritos and cheesecakes, but she refused to listen.

"Everything looks flat when I'm lying on my back," she'd said.

Symphony peered around, and immediately I noticed the look of disgust in her eyes that she tried to disguise once she realized I was watching her.

"What happened to you crashing at your mom's place like you told me you would?" she spoke up, breaking the silence.

I slowly looked away, avoiding eye contact as I shamefully rambled about my mother's disease and whereabouts. Through pitying and sorrowful eyes, Symphony glared at me like her world was coming to an end.

"I'm so sorry, Syren. I didn't know, baby. I'm here for you. I got you," she assured me in an attempt to lift my dampened spirits. She pulled me into her chest, and without resisting, I followed suit. I was tired of being strong. It was hard being strong when you lacked the strength to do so. I sobbed like a baby, capitalizing on the rare moment until my lids grew heavy. Symphony comforted me until the tears and sniffles ceased.

"Let's go get something to eat," she requested.

"I'm drained, girl. Between work and all that damn crying, I'm not feeling it," I expressed while slowly undressing.

"I'll get us something delivered through UberEats. What do you have a taste for?"

"You know I'm not picky. Nah, I want some Chinese food."

"Bet, I got you," Symphony assured, peering down at her phone.

"I'm going to jump in the shower so I can be done before the food gets here." I strutted to the restroom dressed in a bra and panties. I wondered if Symphony was eyeing my fat ass. Afraid to turn around and meet her lustful gaze, I stepped inside, closing the door behind me. Although me and Symphony were girls, she did admit that she was attracted to me before our bond strengthened, but after getting to know me, she looked at me like family. But you can never be too sure.

The hot water felt amazing descending down my body as thoughts of Sir'Mahd surfaced again. Why couldn't I get this dude out of my head? If only he knew the effect he had on me even with no form of intimacy expressed or exchanged.

I stepped out of the shower dressed in a simple nightgown. I would have rather worn a tank top and pajama pants, but I didn't want to step out half-dressed and unintentionally entice her.

"Let's take a selfie to send to RaKeisha. She's going to be so happy, especially when she sees you."

"Hell yeah, come on," I agreed, tossing the cheap bundles over my shoulder.

Symphony took four or five pictures in a matter of seconds.

"I like those two." I pointed at her screen.

"Cool with me." She shrugged, tapping on the Jpay app to send the pictures right away.

"Hey, since I'm on here, do you want me to tell her something?" she asked.

Although it seemed as if I was thinking of what to say, I was really thinking about Symphony and Ra'Keisha's bond. They dealt with one another because of me, but they were never really fond of one another.

"Syren?"

"Huh? My bad. Tell her to try and call me next week. My phone should be set up and I love her so much."

There was a knock on the door.

"I got it," I said, forcing Symphony to sit back down.

"Here." She held out a twenty dollar bill.

"I'm not broke, Symphony."

"Shut up, Syren, I know that. It's my treat."

My eyes bucked once I opened the door and spotted Draco on the other side with our food in her hands. She was still sexy as ever.

"Syren?" She scowled in disbelief.

"Draco, w-what? I mean, I haven't seen you in forever."

She smirked while eyeing me desiriously. "You still so sexy to me, Syren."

"So this how you feeding your fam?" I asked.

"Well, a few months after you got arrested, I was arrested and sentenced to a year in state jail. I picked up a petty misdemeanor not too long ago and my P.O. on my neck about getting a job, so I chose this. It's just another cover-up, if you know what I mean," she said, turning around and tossing her head in the direction of the cranberry G-wagon parked in the middle of the lot.

I slowly nodded my head.

"You visiting, or is this how you living?"

"Nah, this how I'm living for now."

"What? Tae got you living like this?" she asked, appearing shocked.

"Tae?" I had never told Draco about Tae. All she knew was that I was married to Tae's brother.

She smirked, peering at me like she knew something I didn't. "The day you turned yourself in, I was in the lot across the street. There were a few things I wanted to let you know, but once I saw you and Tae locking lips, I changed my mind. I was gon' hold you down to the ground then make you my wife, but that sight alone made my heart turn cold."

"It ain't too cold. You still standing here." Remembering Symphony I held out the twenty dollar bill. "Here. I'm spending time with an old friend. Me and you could make arrangements some other time."

"That's cool. Keep that shit." She was referring to the money as she handed me the food, then walked away.

"Bitch, we might have to warm this shit up," Symphony joked after I shut the door.

"My bad. I almost forgot you were here."

Symphony and I reminisced on the good times we had when we were in prison, short and long term goals, and our personal life until we fell asleep.

***

As I stood over the gas stove whipping the contents inside the Pyrex pot, I could hear the ladies whispering and mumbling things behind me, which was something I was used to. I was always left out of the conversation. It didn't bother me. Lately my mind had been running rapidly. I needed the time to myself and thoughts.

Feeling someone palm my ass, I spun around quickly, shoving Tonya into the cabinets.

"Whoa! Chill, chick. I was just wondering if it was as soft as it looks."

"But you don't fuck with me and I don't fuck with you like that, so keep your hands to yourself," I shot back seriously, suddenly cautious.

"Chill, for real. Honestly I was about to ask your feisty ass something. I just didn't want no one else in my business, so I got a little close."

Glaring at her, I exhaled deeply before looking away. "What's up, Tonya?" I continued to whip. I didn't even bother to give her eye contact as she stood on the side of me.

"I been watching you, Syren. No gay shit."

"And?"

"You be on ya grind like it's a goal or a certain quota you have to meet. I have a proposition for you."

"Shoot."

"What if I told you I could show you how to make another three hundred bucks?"

Instantly my brow rose. Now she was speaking my language.

"How is that? I'm listening."

"These niggas paid. A few grams isn't shit to them. I just skim what I want off top," she admitted confidently.

"You not scared they'll find out?"

"Nope, been doing it for years."

"How do you hide it with them frisking us like that?"

Her eyes roamed past me. I turned around to see what she was looking at.

"What?" I asked, confused.

"Your hair. I put it under the cap beneath my wig."

I thought of the entire procedure and smirked when I recalled the three of them slanging and whipping their heads back and forth when all along it was full of dope.

"Give me just a few days to think about it. It sounds good, but right now I can't let nothing come in the way of my money."

"Then make some."

"I am!" I shot back sternly.

Tonya smacked her lips before walking off.

"She scared. She not trying to do shit," I heard her tell the other two.

"Bitch, I ain't scared," I spoke up.

"You not with the shit either!" Tonya shot back, grabbing her belongings.

"I am with the shit. I'm just not with that shit."

They were out of sight before I finished my sentence, but I was certain they heard me because I surely raised my voice. Even if I did fuck with them, I wouldn't do any dirt with 'em. None of them were to be trusted, especially Tonya's bitch ass.

I listened to the music that blasted from my airpods. Instead of putting them in my ear, I placed them on the counter. In the profession I was in, I needed to be able to see and hear everything.

"Fam, those things should be here next week."

"Bet," King spoke into his phone. "Girl, I forgot you was here," he said, looking startled.

"You know I'm always last. I'll be done in about ten minutes."

"Cool. Hey, you coming to my, um, my party?" King asked, scratching his head.

"Nah, I'm going to be here. I did hear about it though."

"Damn, so you'd rather be here?" He appeared startled as wrinkles formed across his forehead.

"I mean, don't at least one of us have to be here?"

"Nah, I told Tonya to tell y'all that all of you can slide through and show a nigga some love."

"I thought it was supposed to be a surprise?"

"Yeah, I guess it was, but my boy Sir just can't hold water. But check this, if you want to work you can. This line of business is 24/7," he continued

"Nah, I don't think I——"

"Before you say no, I know you like Boosie Badazz. Him and Mo3 are going to perform," King chimed in.

"Oh yeah? Now that's a go."

***

Uh'Nija

I sat in the doctor's office waiting for him to return. I'd been tested for COVID-19 as well as a pregnancy test. I didn't know what was occuring, but the feeling was definitely unfamiliar.

"Ms. Marshall?"

"Yes?" I peered up at him through pleading eyes.

"You're pregnant."

"Oh Lord, this can't be."

After years of fucking with Maine, many nights I prayed to one day have his seed. Now that there was a fifty percent chance the baby looming inside of me might be his, I wished I could just snap my fingers to make everything disappear, including me.

Tobias wasn't an ordinary guy. He had another side to him that I'd never witnessed and did not want to. His stiff demeanor and the chills he sent down my arm every time he looked at me through those beady eyes, no humor whatsoever... I couldn't tell either of the two I was pregnant. I was going to have to be extra careful around Tobias's observant ass.

The Gates and Mo3 lyrics played at a low volume as I thought about Maine's selfish ass. Since leaving him to do as he pleased, I'd been spending a lot of time with Tobias. You would think I lived there. From clothes to feminine products, his and hers décor, and linens, you could definitely notice the difference. I was feeling Tobias. I honestly thought he would take my mind off Maine, but that had yet to happen. I still found myself thinking of Maine quite often. If I wasn't afraid of what Tobias would do if he found out, I'd contact Maine every time I had the urge too. I guess my fears had strengthened me in a way as well.

Killing the engine, I gripped the steering wheel, burying my head slightly above the horn. Tears welled in my eyes as I tried not to let them fall. I felt so alone. I did truly miss Kreesha...and Syren. I needed to talk to someone about the fetus growing inside of me. I was torn between the idea of keeping the baby or aborting it. knowing if I kept it the strife it would cause. Since the miscarriage, I never wanted anything more than my own child. Maine was no good for me, but I loved him unconditionally, and Tobias was all I ever wanted in a man, but I just couldn't allow myself to love him the way he loved me because I was so busy loving Maine.

I tilted my head back, blinking away the tears before slamming the door on my Lexus shut. The vehicle was courtesy of Tobias. He spoiled me rotten. Everything was new down to the polish on my toes.

"Tobias!" I shouted, closing the door behind me.

"Yeah, bae, I'm in the kitchen!"

I smelled a tasty aroma as soon as I bent the corner. I spotted Tobias behind the counter with his apron and chef hat on, whipping some sort of oily liquid in a frying pan.

"Bae, what are you doing?" I asked, unable to cease the giggles.

"Maria had a dentist appointment," he responded as he continued to whip. "Oh, this funny?" He continued peering at me.

"I'm just not used to seeing you like this, Chef Tobias," I joked.

"Sit down, baby, so we can eat. I'm done. I just had to make us a little sauce for the steaks."

I set my purse on the countertop and took a seat at the dinner table. I rose to my feet and decided to set the table. It was the least I could do. Surprisingly, the food smelled and looked pretty appeasing.

As he made his way to the table with two pans in his hands I admired his swag. His long dreads swung freely underneath the hat. He walked with a waddle, giving that monster between his legs a little breathing room. Tobias placed the steak, scalloped potatoes, macaroni and cheese, fried cabbage, and sweet rolls on my plate before taking a seat across from me.

"Bae, this looks so good. Thank you, zaddy."

Tobias rolled his eyes as he chuckled. "Say grace" he said, closing his eyes and lowering his head.

"Dear Heavenly Father, thank you for this meal we're about to receive and I ask you to bless those who do not have, in Jesus's name I pray, amen."

"Amen"

The steak was juicy and tender, unlike any I'd ever tasted. This man was so skilled, it was unreal.

"So what happeend at the clinic?"

For a split second, my eyes bucked and I nearly choked on my food. Appalled by his accurateness, terror consumed me in an instant.

"What? You have a disease, or are you about to have my seed?"

Although Tobias was focused on his plate of food in front of him, he glanced up at me occasionally. Aware of the consequences that lay ahead if I told the truth, I did what was best for me. I stood up and walked towards Tobias.

"We're having a baby," I announced, wrapping my arms around his neck.

He hesitated for a second before hugging me back. I just hoped it was convincing.

***

Tae

"Bae, can I have fourteen hundred dollars?" Iesha asked, curled up next to me on the sofa.

"For what?" I shot back, quickly frowning at the large request.

"I want a new Birkin bag. Look, bae." She pointed at the screen on her phone.

"Man, bae, come on. You know I'm trying to save for this house." I had plans on purchasing a house and a ring, then proposing the day we moved in. I had close to fifteen thousand put up. De'Kari was plugged in with a real estate agent that had several rent-to-own properties. He requested $12,000 for a nice three-bedroom home in the Houston area. Iesha parent's stayed in Kathy, Texas, which was located on the outskirts of Houston, Texas. Since her release, she had only visited her parents once due to her parole stipulations. Although she loved her parents as much as they loved her, it didn't end the dismay they harbored towards her for discrediting her religion and upbringing by dealing with someone like me and becoming a felon.

Many nights, Iesha mentioned how she missed and wanted to see her parents more often. I truly believed Iesha could mend their shattered relationship if she was closer, which would enable her to spend more time with them. Iesha had no idea we were moving to Houston. She assumed my city meant everything to me, and it didn't. I had to learn at a young age that life is bigger than Dallas. Besides, there was nothing here for me.

My mother and I repaired our relationship, but it'd never be similar to the bond she and Maine had. My relationship with Maine would never be restored since I deliberately fucked the bitch he was in love with. Truthfully, the only person I dreaded leaving was Jaelyn. I'd grown extremely close to my nephew and I loved him as if he came from my womb. I knew it was mutual, and once he found out I was relocating, he'd want to come too.

I peered over at Iesha. The defeated look in her eyes made me reconsider. I hated telling her no.

"I'll be back," I said before disappearing.

I headed to the rear of the apartment where mine and Iesha's room was located. Grabbing the knob on the closet door, I pulled it open then bent down. I retrieved the second box from the bottom and removed the lid. Seeing the brand new black Timbs, I smiled. I had only worn them once. They were the same boots I wore the night me and Iesha went on our first date. I reached inside, pulling out two rolls. I placed the thicker roll back inside, peeled two grand off the smaller one and placed the boots back in there original spot.

"Here mama," I said, flopping down beside her.

"Aww, thank you so much, baby," she spoke with gratitude, wrapping her arms around my neck while planting soft kisses all over my face.

"We can go get it when I make it back. I have to go chat with De'Kari real quick.

"Go holla at De'Kari. I'll just go alone. I'll have something cooked by the time you get here."

"That's my baby." Our lips locked in agreeance as we shared the most passionate kiss that could ever be exchanged between two females. Pulling away from her embrace, I rested my forehead on hers. "I'll see you in a few."

"Okay, Breuntae. I love you."

"I love you too." I left the house and pulled off with anticipation of returning.

***

Bunz, De'Kari and I sat on the plush sofa inside of his two story home. Supposedly, De'Kari had finally orchestrated a plan to get even with Maine and become a part of Jaelyn's life. Since finding out Jaelyn was his seed, Maine threatened to not only kill him, but expose a secret of his that would definitely look appealing to authority. I knew it was something serious because De'Kari bowed down instantly.

"Candy Redd sent the video to my phone. It's raw and uncut, all the evidence we'll need," Bunz added.

"Who is Candy Redd?" I asked, confused.

"My cousin - my sixteen-year-old cousin," she emphasized.

"Oh, I see," I said, nodding my head slowly. "You not going to really go through with it, right?" I asked. It was evident I was a bit shook.

"Hell nah! I'm just trying to let him know we're even and make him come on with it," he assured me. Honestly, Jaelyn missed him too. Every time I saw Jaelyn he inquired about De'Kari. He had no clue De'Kari was his biological father, which everyone managed to keep a secret. We sat there waiting for Maine to answer his phone.

"Hey, what's up?" De'Kari spoke sarcastically.

"Who the fuck is this?"

"Damn, after being boys for so long, you don't remember my voice, bruh?"

"Man, what the fuck you want?" Maine snapped. "You must be ready to die?"He continued.

"Nah, I'm enjoying life right now, but this is what I want you to do."

"Pussy, you not calling any shots."

"Oh, I'm not? Check your inbox then."

"Fuck you! I don't have time to waste on you."

Click!

"He thinks it's a game, but as soon as he opens the message, he'll see that I mean business," De'Kari stated in a low tone.

The phone rang alerting the three of us, but it wasn't the phone that belonged to De'Kari. It was Bunz's jack.

"Hello?" she answered after placing the phone on speaker.

"So you set me up? Huh, bitch!"

"Nigga, watch your tone."

"Oh, you hard 'cause you round that nigga? Your cruddy ass still aint shit I'll——"

De'Kari snatched the phone from Bunz. "You'll what?" he yelled.

Upon hearing De'Kari's voice, Maine's tone changed instantly. "You got it. What is it I can do for y'all? I know it's a reason behind the whole operation."

"Nigga, you know what I want, and that's my son. Only reason I stayed quiet for so long is 'cause your police ass threatened to send me up the road. Play dumb if you want and try that shit now and you gon' be cuffed beside me headed up that bitch."

"You got it, fam. Just give me a couple of hours to say my goodbyes."

"I'm gon' give you a hour. You done had fifteen years to say whatever you wanted. In a hour I'm going to call and you better have him in ya' ride."

Maine hung up the phone before agreeing, but whether he spoke on it or not, he understood very clearly. De'Kari was grinning so hard you could barely see his eyes. The same smile was etched across mine.

"Bunz, go set some shit up!" De'Kari shouted in victory.

I could tell Bunz wasn't too fond of the idea once her smile slowly faded as she peered from me to De'Kari.

"Let's just celebrate tonight, baby," she pleaded.

"Baby? Come on now, Bunz, and quit playing with me"

"Oh I'm not good enough to be formally introduced to li'l Jaelyn?" she asked, throwing her hands in the air, clearly frustrated.

"Bitch, you just a bitch. You done fucked and sucked a thousand dicks. Quit buggin'."

The look Bunz gave me expressed the hurt De'Kari caused with his sharp and hostile words. I returned an empathetic gaze before lowering my head.

"Come on, Bunz, you a gutta bitch. Cut all that weak shit out and put sum' in motion so we can run up a check," De'Kari voiced, unmoved by Bunz emotions.

"I'm not even in my car," she whined.

"You're never in your car. Call one of them niggas to come scoop you and quit acting new to this shit!"

My phone rang. I looked down and, seeing Iesha's name, I walked deeper into the house. "Hello?" I answered.

"Hey baby! I was just calling to tell you I'm leaving the mall now."

"Okay, I'll be home in about an hour, maybe sooner."

"Cool. I love you."

"I love you too." I ended the call while heading towards the kitchen. De'Kari and Bunz had lowered their voices and all I could hear was faint whispers. I figured whatever they were, discussing it was between them. I was about to barge in to cease their conversation but as I got closer, I heard Maine's name.

" I don't even know why you frontin' on a bitch like you forgot. I told you we were going to hit Maine!"

"Well how are we supposed to do that when he's onto you now?"

"Don't worry about it. I always come through, don't I?"

"You do. So what's the plan?"

I gripped the handle on the burner that was tucked inside the waist of my Fendi jeans. I pulled it out slowly as I breathed deeply through flared nostrils.

"So you think I'm gon' sit here and let you rob my brother?" I bent the corner, gun in hand aimed directly at De'Kari.

"Whoa! Lil Tae, what's the problem?" De'Kari asked through bulging eyes.

"Y'all motherfuckas not slick. I could hear y'all in here plotting on my brother."

"We been plotting. You didn't have a problem then."

"That was minor to get Jaelyn back. I knew nothing about robbing. Nigga, it's levels to this shit."

"It's levels to this shit," De'Kari mocked in a squeaky voice. "Okay, gangsta, what you gon' do about it then, bitch?" he continued with a testy and defying tone.

Boc! Boc!Boc! Boc! Boc!

I pumped lead into De'Kari's body with each step I took, forcing his body to jerk. Bunz stood in the corner glaring at me in shock. I lifted my burner and aimed it at her. Surprisingly, she was calmer than I thought.

"Where ya tool at?" I questioned.

"Right here," she said, lifting her tight fitted Armani Exchange shirt, revealing the chrome and black Glock.

"Why didn't you help ya mans?"

"He wasn't loyal to me. De'Kari is for self. We can get this money together. I like how you rock," she admitted without hesitation.

"I don't know if I can trust you, ma."

She pulled her burner from her waist and hovered over De'Kari's lifeless body.

Boc! Boc! Boc!

She sent three bullets into his face before tucking her gun inside the waist of her jeans.

"Come on. Let's get out of here!"

***

Syren

I used the back of my hand to wipe the tears from my eyes before grabbing the handle to the door on my late model Honda Civic. At that given moment, I made up in my mind that I wouldn't visit my mother again unless I was coming to pick her up and take her home with me. Today, she cried like a newborn baby fresh out the womb when I stood to leave. It shattered my heart into a thousand pieces, but I couldn't blame anyone but myself. I wasn't physically stable enough to bring her home, nor was she mentally stable enough to lodge in the motel room alone. Since the Foot Locker incident, I hadn't been able to see or talk to Jaelyn.

My phone rang. "What's up?" I answered.

"What's wrong? Has your ass been crying?"

"No!" I lied.

"Are we still going to see Boosie and M03 tonight?"

"Yeah! I'm on my way home. Pull up."

On the way to the room, I tried phoning Draco. I had been calling her phone for at least three days now. I was really looking forward to her filling this void. If I had a choice it would be Sir'Mahd, but he was something like a ghost. I hadn't seen him or anyone like him since the day I was invited into his home. For now, Draco would do. Surprisingly, she answered.

"Hello," she answered in a panic-stricken tone.

"You alright?"

"Yeah, a friend of mine bonded me out and I was released about an hour ago."

"Got out? Are you serious, Dra——"

"Look, before you do all of that, let me explain. Once I get settled and dressed, I'm gon' head your way."

"Okay. Look, I wanted you to come with me to the club tonight. Boosie and M03 going to be there."

"Okay, I'll be there in about two hours."

Later that night

"Mask up!" the bouncer yelled as the line of people moved inside the club.

I wasn't tripping on the mask because mine matched my outfit. I led the way inside the club with Draco and Symphony in tow. Immediately, I peered around, looking for King and his crew. Draco wrapped her arm around my waist.

"Let's go to the bar," she whispered into my ear, never releasing her grip. As soon as the beat kicked in, the three of us paused and began to sing along with the lyrics.

Everybody ain't cha friend
Everybody ain't cha potna
Everybody ain't a real one
If I say I gotcha, I gotcha.

The M03 song blasted from the speaker, sending the club into a frenzy.

"Hey, I want two shots of that clear Crown and a——"

"Shot of Hen," Draco chimed in.

"Bitch, it's *live* in here. I haven't been out since I got out," Symphony yelled joyfully over the loud music. She looked beautiful in the black and white Moncler leggings and matching one piece bathing suit that she wore underneath. The waist trainer concealed the fat she didn't want exposed.

The bartender set our drinks in front of us and simultaneously we tossed it back like pros. It felt like someone had dropped a lit match down my throat. The burning sensation vanished quickly. I refused to order another one. Having wasted enough time, I peered around for King and his people.

"Oh shit! There go them boys!" the DJ yelled into the mic.

The crowd began parting like the Red Sea. Symphony ran dead smack in the middle and dropped to her knees.

"Bitch, what are you doing?"

"I'ma tell Boosie to set his dick on my tongue. I just want to taste it," she voiced seriously.

"Symphony, get your crazy ass up and come on. You can do that shit later after the club."

She pouted as she made her way to the side like everyone else.

"You trippin'. You a bad bitch. You don't got to do all of that to get any attention," I spoke closely into her ear.

My eyes grew twice their size when I spotted King and his crew making their way through the club. He looked edible in his Louis Vuitton get-up with the matching phone box. The crowd filed in behind them once the last guy passed. He strolled by confidently as if he should've been first. I stared at him closely, stopping dead in my tracks. His imperious aura pervaded the atmosphere like some sort of spell had been cast. Luckily he made it to the V.I.P. section without glancing in my direction. In spite of his unapproachable and untouchable demeanor, there was definitely something familiar about him. He needed to remove that fucking mask!

"Close your mouth," Draco said, pushing me in the back.

"Damn, my bad!" I apologized, rolling my eyes.

"Bitch, I thought that was Boosie! I'm glad you made me get up, but then again, they whole li'l clique looks pretty appealing. Ain't them ya boys?" Symphony yelled. We had only been at the club thirty minutes and she was already slurring.

"Yeah, the first one is the one that invited me," I answered apprehensively. Somewhere down the line, I had lost confidence.

"Come on then, bitch!" Symphony dragged me towards V.I.P. and I dragged Draco.

As soon as I emerged from the crowd that separated their section from the dance floor, King was right there to greet me.

"What's up, baby? You made it! He held out his arms up as he eyed me lustfully.

I wasted no time jogging up the steps and wrapping my arms around his neck. I peered directly into the eyes of Tonya, who stood with Meka, Neko, and a few of the foot soldiers. Tonya's eyes were full of venom and envy. I politely smirked at the bitch.

"You look good, girl, and ya friend do too," he said, looking past me at Symphony. "My bad, fam, you want a drink?" King asked Draco, who stared back at him like he had poop on his face. Damn, Sy. Ya people good?" he scowled, mugging Draco.

I didn't understand where the animosity had come from, but Draco needed to chill. I don't know what I was thinking inviting her, knowing the niggas was going to be in here thick. Truthfully, I didn't give a fuck if Draco was mad, sad, or all of the above. I was checking for one nigga and one nigga only, and that was Sir.

Beat King blasted through the speakers. Meka got into her stance and started bouncing her ass in front of the guy that unintentionally made me and every other bitch in the club feel some type of way. Even though I didn't know dude, it felt like I did, and jealousy consumed me instantly. Meka was throwing her ass like dudes were throwing money.

That gotta be zaddy, I thought.

I gawked at the guy I assumed to be "Sir" from a distance. Once we made eye contact, he waved me over. I looked to the left at Tonya's nosy ass because I knew she was watching my every move.

"Ole basic-ass bitch."

She was dressed in a black sweater dress with matching pumps. Not only did he wave me over, but he just dismissed her friend, tapping her on the shoulder and whispering in her ear. If that alone didn't make the bitch want to fight me, my swag had her ready to behead me. The form-fitting Gucci sweater felt like a constant hug, and so did the denim jeans that made my ass look twice its normal size and complemented the Gucci knee high boots that stopped right above my knee. The boots were tight around my legs, practically hugging them, making my thighs appear bigger.

He reached out and grabbed me. His scent assaulted my nostrils instantly. *That scent, I've smelled it before*, I thought. *But where?* I continued.

Boom! Boom! Boom!

"Syren!" I heard Symphony yell.

I snapped out of my trance, broke from his grasp, and found my friend.

"You okay?"

"Yes, I'm good. You good?"

"Yeah, come on."

I grabbed her hand and flew out the emergency exit door. Panic-stricken, I looked left and then right, unsure of which way to go as the cool weather engulfed me, compelling my teeth to chatter.

"Come on!" Draco yelled, standing beside her car. You could tell she was about to pull off. Half her body was in and the top half was out as she waved us over. Afraid more shots would ring out, I took off like a track star at a track meet.

"Y'all good?" she asked as soon as me and Symphony hopped in.

"Yeah. Let's go," I urged. I stared out the window, upset and glad all at the same time. I was ecstatic to still be alive, but I was slightly vexed on another missed opportunity. If me and Sir didn't cross paths soon, I surely wouldn't mind getting to know King's friend.

"Damn, I didn't get to see Boosie and M03!" I yelled, slamming my hand down on the leather interior.

"Hit my shit again and you'll never see them niggas!"

Draco was right. I had no idea what came over me, but I was trippin' hard.

The next morning I awoke to a note from Draco and a snoring Symphony.

I can't say I enjoyed myself last night, but I did enjoy being in your presence. Have a good day. I'll get with you later.
Draco

I stepped over a sleeping Symphony, who was sprawled out on the floor next to the bed. The time on my phone read 10:15 a.m. I rushed over to the sink. I had to be at work at 12. Since purchasing the car I had no reason to be late, but after last night I was pretty sure I wouldn't be the only one dragging in. I turned on the hot water in the shower, then peered around the tiny motel room.

"I'm sick of this life," I whispered. There was nothing definite that I was looking for as I continued to look around.

I grabbed my robe, hung it on the bathroom door, then hopped in the shower. My mind roamed rapidly as the hot water descended down my back. Tears came to my eyes as I thought about my only child. What did I do for him to hate me so much? Truly I just wanted to be in his presence. I wanted things to be how they were before the incarceration, but the reality is, they're not. In a way I took my frustration out on my skin as I scrubbed my body until it was too painful for me to continue. I stepped out and grabbed my robe from atop of the door.

"Oh, you done finally woke your ass up?" I asked Symphony who had sat up, rubbing the boogers from her eyes.

"What time is it?"

"Almost eleven."

"Eleven? Shit, I have to go!"

"I thought you were off today?"

"I am. I just don't sleep this late."

"Oh, okay, yeah, I'm about to leave too. Hey, have you heard from Ra'Keisha?"

"Nah. Honestly, she had been waiting to see pictures of you and that's really why I sent those, but you know me and her still don't fuck with each other like that."

"Well, she'll be very grateful you sent those pics."

"I mean, I'm out now. It doesn't matter if she fucks with me or not."

"Don't be like that, Symphony. That's my friend and she's doing a lot of time. She needs people like us. You know in the bible it says, 'Remember those in prison as if you were in there'."

"Come on, Sy. Honestly, I don't know why you fuck with her like that anyways. She grimy and she's not to be trusted."

"Don't do that, Symphony, Ra'Keisha is my girl too and I'm not going to listen to you talk shit about her. I'm a lot of things, but fake isn't one."

"Bitch, I know you not fake. That's why I fucks with you. But I can respect it. I'll see you later. I'm about to head out so I won't be late for my hair appointment." Dressing quickly, Symphony almost fell trying to slide into her skinny jeans.

"I love you, girl, be careful," I said, standing by the door as she walked out. We shared a hug and a peck on the cheek. "Call me," I added before closing the door.

I thought bringing Draco back into the equation would satisfy me enough to rid Sir'Mahd from my thoughts. I was wrong! Dude was in my fucking dreams last night and on my mind as soon as I opened my eyes. Last night reminded me of how I felt the first time I met Sir'Mahd. Only difference is this time, I wasn't going to let him slip away so easily.

I cleaned up around the room and then got dressed. Minutes later, I was closing the front door to my telly dressed in a dark grey maxi dress, bare ass cheeks, and a pair of silver MK sandals that I purchased from the clearance rack at Nordstrom. I stopped by the front office to see if I had any mail before leaving.

"Hey, I got something, Mr. Jimmy?"

"Sure, come on in," he answered sharply, acting as if he wasn't just asleep.

I strolled inside while he sorted through the mail. The nineteen inch plasma played highlights from last night's game on ESPN. I couldn't wait to purchase a seventy-two inch and watch sports. During my little stint ,I had become a true sports fan.

"Here you go," he said, handing me the thick stack of mail.

Immediately I flipped through it, looking for one in particular, and there it was. I dashed out the office and into my car. I ripped the letter open from Ra'Keisha.

Hey friend,

Words cannot be formed to express how much I miss you. The little time we spent meant so much to me and most importantly, I appreciate you keeping your word. Symphony sent pics trying to rub shit in, on the cool. But no fucks are given on my end 'cause now I have pictures of your beautiful ass. You know I'm still fucking with Melanie. Her people got that bread so she pays how she weigh. You need a-n-y-t-h-i-n-g, let me know. I got you. Just 'cause I'm doin' a lot of time, you still and forever will be on my mind and just a letter away. Set that phone up soon as you can.

P.S. Symphony is not to be trusted. I know that's ya girl, but I just don't want you to learn the hard way. Head up, breasts out. I love you.

Tears smeared the blue lines on the notebook paper. I smiled as I envisioned Ra'Keisha laughing and joking like we used to.

The other day I paid Rhonda a visit to obtain Maine's number.

"Hey," I spoke once he answered.

"Who is this?"

"Syren. Can I speak to Jaelyn?"

"You have the wrong number, li'l momma."

"Okay, th-thanks."

I found it pretty odd that Maine's own mother would have the wrong number but then again, she could've simply flat out lied.

I killed the engine and hopped out. I was a few minutes late, but it wasn't nothing compared to the time I'd show up before I had a car.

"What's up, King?" I greeted him, stepping inside.

"Damn, you could've at least called and checked on a nigga," he said, throwing his hands in the air.

"You could've called and checked on a bitch," I shot back.

King laughed, closing the door behind me. He sat on the couch. As I headed towards the back I switched my hips a little harder, sure he was watching.

"Hey girl!" Tonya yelled as soon as I entered.

I peered at her, dumbfounded, before slowly looking at the others. "What's up, Tonya?" I mumbled, placing my bag on the counter.

"You have fun last night? I'm glad no one got hurt. I wish I knew who that crazy motherfucker was that was shooting."

"Yeah, I had fun before all of that bullshit. Honestly, you didn't look too happy to see me. I just knew today you were going to be in your feelings."

"Feelings? Oh, never that. I put those beneath my feet and walk on them motherfuckas. I'm just glad you and your people made it out safely. What I do want to know is, who was that stud chick that was with you?"

"Draco? She's a friend of mine," I responded dryly. I didn't want to reveal too much because I didn't trust Tonya's ass. King could've put her up to asking me. Who knows?

"Oh, okay," she added.

I assume she caught my drift because she didn't bother me for the remainder of the day until it was close to time for us to go. Tonya had been moving abnormally fast, yet I still managed to keep up. Usually I'd be extremely behind, but as they were getting stripped out, I had just finished and was cleaning up. Whoever was last had to clean and straighten everything up. Cleaning up had been my duty since I started, but it didn't bother me at all. During the time alone, I meditated and conversed with God, something I promised myself to always do once I had gotten released.

"Okay, King, I'm ready," I announced after sighing deeply. I placed my purse, sandals, bra, and dress on the table as I stood in front of King with my back to him. Arms up and legs spread, I stood still as he closely observed me.

"Lift ya feet, wiggle ya toes," he directed. "Bend over, spread ya ass cheeks," he continued. He slid a finger in my pussy from the back, felt around my box, then pulled out.

I stood there patiently as he searched my belongings one at a time and I got dressed. He poured everything out of my bag onto the table. As soon as I, then he, spotted the drugs, my heart fell to my toes.

***

Tobias

"If you don't trust her, why are you with her? Why am I never enough for you, Tobias?"

"Lower your voice, Maria, and quit questioning me," I spoke gravely, peering into her woeful eyes.

Maria and I had been fucking for years, but it was never anything more than sex, and I never gave her reasons to believe otherwise. Maria wasn't really attractive, but she did possess comely features that over time I couldn't resist. Seemingly she was just my maid, but I believe wholeheartedly that Maria would die for me. I've always been a man of few- few words, few chances, few friends, few family, etc. However, when it comes to my family, I only kept in contact with my mother. I had no knowledge of the identity of my real father and I barely dealt with my mother. I'm blessed in many ways. Financially was one of them. I didn't mind giving. but I refused to be used.

"I'm sorry. Tobias."

"Don't be."

Uh'Nija didn't know that I lied about Maria being at a dentist appointment. I just couldn't understand why the news upset her so much. I had a recording device placed inside Uh'Nija's car when I purchased it. The ceaseless sniffles and displeased grunts had me ponding on the reasoning for it all, but there were so many different ideas consuming my thoughts.

"She's lying about something. I just can't figure it out."

"Do you love her, Tobias?"

I peered up at a humorless Maria who was looking at me through squinted eyes. " Yes, I do."

Maria used the back of her hand to swipe away the tears that immediately fell. She looked into my eyes and said, "Okay. I'll find out." She turned to walk away.

"Maria," I voiced, ceasing her steps.

"Yes, Tobias?" she answered, turning her head to the side.

"Come here", I demanded, standing to my feet.

I met her halfway, forcefully grabbing the back of her head, bringing her closer as I pressed my lips against hers. She parted her mouth and I shoved my thick tongue down her throat. Our tongues clashed, then caressed. My mans stiffened. Sweet moans escaped her mouth as we stood in the center of my study, fondling each other and kissing. I almost forgot Uh'Nija was upstairs sleeping. I just hoped she would stay that way because there was no way I'd be able to walk away now. It had been a few weeks since I'd been inside Maria. With all the strength in the world I couldn't shake the burning desire that only she could put out.

"Bend over," I demanded, gripping the back of her neck tighter.

She turned around and walked towards the desk. Before positioning herself against it,, she glanced back at me.

"Tobias why are you doing this?" she whispered, distressed and teary-eyed.

Without acknowledging her question, I lifted the skirt, exposing her bare ass, and rammed all nine inches into her opening. She used one hand to cover her mouth to muffle the sound as I continued to plunge my log in and out of her hole. I used my foot to kick her feet farther apart as she leaned against the desk. Grabbing her waist but spreading her ass cheeks at the same time, I roughly penetrated Maria. Her sweet nectar resembled a breath of fresh air, freedom to a man after serving a lengthy bid, I loved this shit. The muscles in my ass began to twitch. I knew what was coming next. I sped up my pace.

"I'm cumming," I whispered.

"Me too, Tobias, baby, me too."

"Get down," I spoke quickly through clenched teeth. I tightened every bone in my body seconds before releasing my semen.

Maria dropped to the floor and tilted her head back as if she was on a beach soaking up the sun. I gripped my penis and sprayed her with cum as if it was a can of Lysol and she was some sort of bacteria.

"Uhhhhh!" I sounded, breathing heavily, barely able to stand.

She rose to her feet, bent down, kissed the tip of my penis, then walked out of my study.

I'm glad she did so without me telling her to, but come to think of it, our sexual gatherings always ended like that.

***

Maine

"I'm spending time with my son. Go ahead and hold shit down. I'll be through there in a few days," I instructed Reggie.

"No problem, fam. You know I got you. Take your time and enjoy yourselves, everythang good," he responded. I could hear the excitement in his voice.

Click!

With everything I had going on, I didn't have time to trip on his position. I just hated that I was forced into leaving him in charge of so much. Spending time with Jaelyn was a lie. He begged me to go over his friend's house after school and I agreed to pick him up later. For three days he had been only able to go to school and back.

I hadn't heard from De'Kari since the sudden call and honestly, he had me shook. To know Cocoa and Candy Redd set me up was a slap to the face. To think that I fucked up the slight stability I had with Uh'Nija for that bitch angered me to the extreme. If I was cuffed, I could kill that bitch with my feet. Time and time I fucked over Uh'Nija when truly she was the one too good to a nigga. I figured De'Kari had been trying to reach me, but I changed my number. I knew if he really wanted to find me he could, but I refused to give up my son so easily. Blood don't have to solidify shit. That's my seed and I'm willing to die before another nigga got in his head and made him believe anything different.

Bored out of my mind, I flopped on the sofa. I figured I'd watch the fight Jaelyn ordered the other night since I never got a chance to see it. I scrolled through recently purchased PPVs and clicked on the most recent one.

Confused and in pure disbelief, I peered at the screen until the toast, eggs, and pan sausages came flying out of my mouth uncontrollably, decorating my black leather sofa. Clutching my aching stomach, I crawled to the trash bin and continued to throw up inside of it. Moans and grunts blasted through the speakers on the sixty-four inch TV, upsetting me even more. Sweat profusely descended down my forehead as I began to hyperventilate. This shit was unreal.

"My son?" I mumbled, peering up at the ceiling. I didn't get a response, but immediately my mind went back to a day I'd never forget.

Five years ago...

"Did you decide where we're going?" Syren asked, putting away the dishes that Jaelyn and his friends used to eat ice cream and cake out of.

Syren and I had spent most of the day shopping and treating Jaelyn and his friends on his eleventh birthday. Now we were headed out to have more fun.

"Jaelyn wanted to go to Dave and Buster's," I responded, giving her a hand.

"Okay, go get him. By the time you get back, I'll be done," Syren assured, moving quickly. Jaelyn had been instructed to shower and get dressed.

"Jaelyn!" I hollered, proceeding down the hallway. I peered into the restroom and inside his room, but there was no sign of Jaelyn. Wrinkles formed across my forehead as I stood in the middle of the hallway, confused. I checked mine and Syren's bedroom and to my surprise, I spotted Jaelyn. I smiled, seeing him struggling as he reached for my cologne. I stayed silent, curious to see which fragrance he would choose, but once I spotted him grab Syren's tube of lipstick and slowly apply it, I became enraged. Visions of me choking and beating him flashed before my eyes. But as I looked at his puny body I knew I had to reconsider. If not, I'd mistakenly kill him.

"Put that lipstick down," I spoke through scrunched lips and clenched teeth.

He jumped at the sound of my voice while the tube of lipstick went flying. "Sorry, D-dad," he apologized, picking the tube up and placing it on the counter.

With each passing second I peered at him I grew angrier, seeing the red lipstick poorly applied across his small lips. Snatching him by his collar, I pushed him into the restroom with enough force to make him fall to his knees.

"Wash that shit off," I demanded, peering at him through stoic eyes.

"Yes sir," he mumbled, scrambling to the sink to get the lipstick off.

"Use soap," I said after seeing how the red lipstick stained his lips .

"You ready, baby?" Syren yelled from a distance.

"We're coming!" I hollered back.

Jaelyn continued to scrub his lips with his hand as he peered through the mirror at me the entire time. I wiped around the sink once he was done, then knelt down to where we were nearly face to face.

"Lipstick is for women; not men. If I ever catch you doing anything that men don't do, or are supposed to do, I'ma tear the skin off your ass. You hear me, boy?" I stated through squinted eyes.

"Yes sir," he answered in a shaky voice.

I placed my hand on the top of his head and guided him out of the restroom and down the hall.

"Y'all ready?" Syren asked, full of excitement.

I responded with a tight-lipped response while Jaelyn shook his head quickly, attempting a forced smile. Syren picked up on the awkward gesture, but remained silent.

During the trip to Dave and Buster's, I was a bit standoffish. My responses were short and dry. To them, I may have appeared irritated. I was contemplating whether or not to tell Syren or keep the incident between Jaelyn and me. Even as a child I didn't want to shame him more than I had already done. With Syren being his mother, she was entitled to know such things, however, his actions shamed me as well as his parents and I refused to speak on it again. To ensure Jaelyn would never repeat what he did today, there were things I must enforce. Although he sounded convincing once he assured me he would never do it again, I couldn't let up so easily because there were no limits to what I'd do to him next time.

I tried to enjoy the games, food, and the presence of the two people I loved wholeheartedly, but my thoughts wouldn't allow me to do so. Every time I looked at Jaelyn, I saw the lipstick. He knew I was upset. His smile would fade every time we'd lock eyes and eventually, he was no longer able to enjoy himself either.

Back at home, Syren tried picking me for information, but I refused to comply.

"Hey, me and Jaelyn will be back. He's growing up, and I think it's time him and I have the talk. Don't wait up. We'll be back in a few hours."

"O-okay." Syren was obviously perplexed, but she agreed anyway.

Jaelyn lay on his bed in a fetal position.

"Come on, Jaelyn, we going for a ride."

He slowly climbed off his full-sized bed, slid into his Reebok Classics, and headed out the door with me leading the way. I removed a bottle of Hen from underneath my seat and filled both styrofoam cups halfway. I added Coke to one but left the other as is.

"Grab that cup right there, son. Sip slow and don't spill it," I instructed.

"Oooh, soda! Thanks, Dad," he said, gulping the drink. "Mmmmmm," he moaned loudly, squeezing his eyes shut tight as the veins protruded from his neck .

"I told you to sip slow," I said while smirking.

He peered at me unblinkingly as he clutched his chest to subdue the burning in his small chest.

Thirty minutes and two cups of Henny and Coke later, Jaelyn was sound asleep in the passenger seat. It had been years since I had been in the game, but I was still well-respected as if I had never left. There was no problem whatsoever getting Jaelyn into the strip club.

"What's up, Maine?" Duffy asked as soon as I approached the entrance. Immediately he scowled at Jaelyn. I handed him the hundred dollar bill and with the other hand. He held it above his head similarly to a surrender before saying, "You got it," and stepping to the side.

I guided Jaelyn through the club with my hand resting atop of his head. He appeared entranced as I led him to V.I.P. I wasn't my usual self. I bypassed many women who called my name or grabbed my dick in the process. Usually I'm very amiable and flirty, but not tonight I had things other than pleasure of any form on my mind.

"Bella, come here!" I yelled over the loud music to the thin waitress.

"Yes, Maine?"

"Bring me a bottle of Henny and tell Dimples to come here," I requested before sitting next to Jaelyn on the sofa.

He peered up at me, but was too afraid to inquire.

Dimples strutted toward us quickly and immediately wrinkles formed across her forehead as she spotted a nervous Jaelyn. Smoothly, I motioned for her to come to me.

"Give him the green light," I requested. She was a bit hesitant at first until she spotted the two hundred dollar bills in my hand.

She stuffed them in her breasts then said, "How old is he, Maine?"

"Eleven."

She nodded her head in agreement before clamping her arms around Jaelyn's neck. She rolled her hips and popped her kitty to the beat while Jaelyn peered at her unblinkingly. She turned around, grabbing her ankles, and made her ass clap while looking back at him. Sweat beads formed across Jaelyn's forehead as he began to pinch his armpits. Dimples slowly fell back onto his small lap and grinded on and against him until he was fully erect. Smoothly, she unzipped his zipper and slid down onto him. Shortly, his body shook violently and Dimples zipped up his jeans before climbing off. We shared a wink and then she disappeared.

"You good li'l man?"

He quickly nodded as we bumped fists.

Present day

Although that was the first time I physically handled the matter with Jaelyn, it wasn't the first time I had spoken to him about appearing too feminine. I griped and grilled him when he would be too affectionate with Syren at a young age. "I know that's your momma, but all that kissing and hugging for little girls," I stated only a few times before he completely stopped. Recounting the past, I did everything I could and then some to prevent him from lusting after things similar to the shit I had just seen on the TV, but it didn't change nothing. This time, Jaelyn had gone too far.

Tae

Reality didn't punch me in the face until I received the text from Iesha.

"Where u at? U suppose 2 got here a hr. ago"

I slid the phone into my joggers and continued to count the money. Before leaving completely out of De'Kari's spot, Bunz doubled back and took the money, guns, and drugs he had stashed.

Blunt dangling from my mouth, I sat on the edge of the bed with just a Fila sports bra and matching joggers. There was so much going on. I had to get comfortable to concentrate. Bunz, on the other hand, was too comfortable, if you ask me. She was dressed in nothing but a thong. She paraded around the room weighing and bagging the dope and checking the clips on the sticks. Although she was practically naked, appearing as though she was seeking attention, she paid me no mind. She rarely looked up unless I called her name.

"So what's the plan?" I asked, completely still as I peered into her direction. Bunz's body was flawless. I tried to look into her eyes and not at her plump breasts or voluptuous ass, but it was a challenge.

"What do you mean? We resume normal activity."

"You don't think the cops can tie us into anything, huh?"

"I hope not, but if so… Tae, just hold your own. I'm not going to give them pigs a statement 'cause even then the results are the same."

"You sound like you've been through something like this before," I said, peering at her intently, eyes casually roaming over her assets.

"I have. That's why I knew what I knew at a young age. I fucked up and said the wrong thing, so I know where that route takes you as well, but, the bottom line is to stay silent. There's a ninety percent chance they might take us in for questioning, so if they do, act incompetent and ask for your lawyer."

I listened to Bunz carefully while she rambled on. I had been in some tough situations, but nothing to this extent. She sounded so convincing and I wanted to trust her, but I learned at a young age that a pair of lips will tell you anything. Until this shit blew over, I planned to keep her as close as possible so that I could monitor everything down to her conversations.

The growling sound that came from my stomach snapped me from my thoughts. "You hungry?"

"Hell yeah," she replied, spinning around.

"What you have a taste for?"

"Um, breakfast."

"Uber Eats?" I suggested.

"Nah, I don't think that's a good idea. No one needs to know where we lay our head."

"You right."

"Yeah, I want pancakes, hash browns, sa——"

"You coming with me?" I chimed in unblinkingly.

She smirked before tracing her lips with her tongue. "So this is how it's going to be?" she asked.

"Call it what you want to call it," I nonchalantly replied

"Cool. Just know the feeling is mutual. Let's go."

I didn't even bother to respond to that slick shit she was spittin'. I just wanted something to eat. Bunz quickly got dressed and we left the room together.

Denny's was just ten minutes away. We ordered our food and headed back. The ride there and back was silent, which at the time went unnoticed because I was such in deep thought. The idea of the charges sticking had me a bit shook, but then again, it was no use pondering or stressing behind spilled milk.

Once we returned, I parked in the same spot I had parked in previously, and quickly but thoroughly surveyed the area before entering the room. I made a mental note to call Iesha once I was done eating. Bunz tossed her keys and purse on the table with a bit of aggression.

"You good?" I asked, sitting on the edge of the bed.

"Yeah," she stated dryly.

I shrugged my shoulders and dug into my food. I didn't have the energy to kiss no one's ass other than my own. After eating my food, I phoned Iesha.

"Hey baby, where are you?" she asked.

"Something came up. I'll explain it once I get there."

"Okay, just hurry up and get here."

"Okay. I'll see you in a little bit," I assured her. I dumped all the contents in one bag, then rose to my feet.

"How would Iesha feel if she saw me asleep on the couch?" Bunz asked, catching me completely off-guard.

"You not, so why would that even be the case?"

"Surely I am if you're leaving," she answered calmly.

"What's the problem with me leaving?"

"Come on, Tae. You not dumb, slow, or illiterate. Those soft, sexy, wet motherfuckas on your face hold the key to my freedom."

"You think I'm a rat?"

"No, I don't *think* you a rat. I actually *think* you're pretty solid, but I don't get paid to *think*. I do *know* what pressure does to the most hardest niggas, so I'd just rather not chance it."

"Fuck it then. We'll get all this shit together and head out tomorrow."

I was so pissed I didn't call Iesha. *What was I going to tell her?* I thought. I removed my sneaks and climbed onto the hard mattress.

Boom!

The extremely loud noise awoke me from my deep slumber. The bright light aiming directly at me was all I could see. I held up my hands and squinted my eyes to see past it and the barrel of the gun came into view.

"Put your hands up where I can see them!" the white officer yelled. His partner flicked the switch to get a better look.

I peered over at a stunned Bunz, who lay next to me. She looked at me and said a few significant words.

"It's time. Be ready."

I nodded in agreement to assure her that I could read her mind. It was as if the officers weren't standing a few feet away pointing drums at our heads. Another cop strolled in wearing just a T-shirt with FEDS on it.

"Y'all can make this easy or hard," he announced, slowly pacing the floor while the other two still had their guns trained on us.

"What's that supposed to mean?" I asked, trying to appear calm, though inwardly I was scared as hell.

"Tell us what happened to De'Kari."

His request startled me. De'Kari hadn't been dead for ten hours and we were already being interrogated.

"We don't know shit!" We both spoke in unison.

"Okay, this is how this is going to go. We confiscating everything - the drugs, money, and guns - but since we didn't come for that, I'll give you a pass on those charges. See ladies, we've been watching De'Kari for a long time, since he and Jermaine were merely corner boys selling nickel and dime rocks."

The sound of my brother's name caused my eyes to widen.

"Bre'untae." He paused. "I'm aware of who you are too," he continued. "However, all of that is beside the point. I know one of you, if not both of you know, what happened to De'Kari. Get dressed so we can figure this all out."

Syren

"What the fuck? For real, Syren?" King asked, peering deeply into my eyes in disbelief.

"I swear I do not know where that came from," I denied shakily.

His eyes were stony and unsparing. I was afraid of his next move. He reached into his pocket and retrieved his phone. He never took his eyes off me as he spoke into the receiver.

"Get here now," was all he said before ending the call.

"Look, King, I swear one of them hoes must've set me up 'cause I wouldn't dare do not shit like that. You've been nothing but good to me," I explained, trying to plead my case.

He didn't respond, he didn't even bother to look at me. He sat down on the sofa across from me, leaving me standing there saddened and bare as the day I came out of my mother's womb.

There was a knock on the door. The banging seemed distant, but it still could easily be heard. King got up and walked around me towards the rear of the house. I quickly slipped on my dress once he disappeared, unsure of what was going to transpire next.

Seeing Sir'Mahd bend the corner took my breath away.

So that's Sir, I thought, recalling the night at the club. It was something about him that was familiar then, but I just couldn't pinpoint it. My heart beat sped up like a junkie who just hit some bad dope. The closer he got the more his eyes narrowed.

"Syren?" he questioned aloud.

"Huh?" I responded, my voice still shivery.

"This is the one that's been stealing. I found these in her bag." King walked to the table and retrieved the rocks.

I peered at Sir'Mahd through pitiful eyes, hoping he'd sense the sincerity and cease the madness. The odd feeling in the pit of my stomach surfaced, and it wasn't because I was afraid. Surely I was, but it happened whenever I was in his presence. Sir'Mahd's, that is. I wondered if he felt what I felt. For a second he appeared torn, but the expression vanished before I could certainly detect it.

"I'm not a thief! I did not steal shit! I can't lose this job! I don't have shit!" I cried out as the snot from my nose dripped onto my lips.

Sir'Mahd peered at King, then at me.

"Get the fuck out! If I see you around my shit, I'ma body ya ass. I'm gon' let you keep ya life, but you done here," he stated before walking out.

I stood there for merely a few seconds looking dumbfounded before King scooped everything off the table into my bag.

"You can have them rocks. Looks like you gon' need them," he commented, pointing towards the door.

I was so hurt that my heart ached. Losing this job meant losing my son and my mother. Maine would never let me have full custody or any custody of Jaelyn without shit, and I certainly couldn't win a custody battle with no stability.

Defeated, I dragged to my car. Once inside, I wailed like a child, then shot a text to Symphony. "Meet me at the room."

Sir'Mahd

109

I was glad to have found one of the culprits who were responsible for taking my shit. But after re-evaluating everything, something still didn't sit right with me. I had to get to the bottom of it. I suspected anyone besides the gorgeous woman that stood in the center of the living room quivering as she appeared extremely spooked. Initially I began to sympathize as I peered at the woman who had consumed my thoughts on a daily since the first time I laid eyes on her. Not only had Syren occupied my thoughts, but she was in a few of my dreams too. Low-key I had been looking for shorty since the day she ran out of my crib, but I had no luck finding her. I quickly snapped out of the trance and focused on the task at hand: business. I was starting to consider her pleas when she said something that vexed my spirit. One thing I hated with a passion was a liar.

"I'm not a thief. I did not steal shit. I can't lose this job. I don't have shit!" I repeated inwardly. I thought back to when I first met Syren when she informed me about her house being built. Getting a house built from the ground up didn't sound like someone who didn't have shit. Either way she had lied, so I definitely couldn't bring myself to believe her now when King had solid proof right before my eyes.

"Get the fuck out! If I see you around my shit, I'ma body ya ass. I'm gon' let you keep ya life, but you done here."

Ever since I spoke those words, they'd been nothing but a pestering, constant reminder. Me and King even celebrated by tossing a few shots back, but even at the time I didn't feel so victorious. I actually felt defeated.

"How can you miss something you never had?" I asked myself repeatedly. My gut feeling and persistent conscience is the reason I was doing twenty miles over the speed limit at seven in the morning to take a look at the tapes. I tossed and turned all last night, wondering if I truly made a mistake.

As soon as I dropped Amyah off at school, I headed into King's direction. I didn't bother phoning King. I parked in the front, jogged around back, and let myself in through the back door. Grunts and indistinct chatter could be heard from a distance as soon as I entered through the rear. I was about to yell King's name to obtain his attention, but now I was curious to know exactly what was occuring. I followed the noise and the closer I got, the cleared the chatter became.

"Yeah, eat that dick."

I couldn't tell if it was King's voice or one of the younger cats. I opened the bathroom door. It was empty. I proceeded down the hall towards one of the three bedrooms. I opened the first door to the left and instantly spotted Tonya on her knees sucking King, who stood against the wall in the bedroom. He appeared to be using the wall for some sort of leverage. I had heard a while ago just how "fiya" Tonya's head was. I thought they would stop, but they only paused until they realized it was just me. Tonya simply peered at me while she sucked King and he closed his eyes and continued to enjoy the lip service.

"Don't mind me," I joked before closing the door.

I headed towards the master bedroom, which was located closer to the front. I peered at the movement on the screens and chuckled lightly after spotting King and Tonya again. A part of me couldn't believe King had become another one of Tonya's victims. The tape only held seven days worth of footage, so I rewinded it back seven days ago.

Uh'Nija

I watched Tobias back out of the driveway just to assure he left. Tears descended down my face immediately. I was beyond distressed. I had begun to feel like a prisoner in my own home. No family, no friends, just my seed that was growing inside of me. I was growing despondent and detached as the days passed. I guess you can call it bittersweet because I knew for certain that if I had this baby and it was not Tobias's he'd surely spazz.

"Ooh, I'm sorry, Mees Unija," Maria apologized after barging inside. "I thought you left with Mr. Tobias. I was coming to clean"

"You can come in." I neared the door. "I was just about to make me something to eat," I said, opening the door.

111

"There's no need for that. It's hot food on the stove," she spoke.

I had no idea Maria could speak such good English. I never heard her talk so much. I paused before responding as I peered at her, slightly confused.

"Mees Unija, have you been crying?"

"I'm fine, Maria. I'm just starving," I lied.

She took a deep breath then said, "It's Tobias, isn't it? You don't have to lie to me. I've been around quite a minute. I've seen that man make many beautiful women like yourself fall to their knees."

Tears fell rapidly as Maria's words pierced my soul.

"I love Tobias, but I'm a woman just like you and it hurts me to see you hurting," she expressed with such emotion, as if she had been in my shoes before.

I leaned into her chest and wailed like a baby. She caressed my shoulders and upper back while my tears soaked her T-shirt.

"Just lay down, Unija. I'll bring you your meal in bed."

I didn't pull back immediately. I attempted to cease the sniffles, but it wasn't as easy as I thought it'd be. The breakdown was long overdue.

Slowly I lifted my head off her shoulder, quickly wiping the tears from my eyes and cheeks. I dragged myself to the bed and flopped down. As Maria's words replayed in my head I scooted to the top of the bed and curled up in a fetal position. Moments later, Maria returned with a large tray that held several different plates.

"You have to eat mama," she whispered, hovering over me.

I scooted back, giving her enough room to sit. She placed the tray on the nightstand and sat on the edge of the bed directly in front of me. I couldn't tell what was on the plates, but I could smell seafood. She swiped the buttery shrimp across my lips while begging me to open my mouth. The delicious aroma immediately made my mouth water, and I opened my mouth wide enough to nibble on the bite-sized shrimp. Maria picked up another shrimp off the plate once I was done, only this time she ate it, which startled me because she devoured the shrimp so seductively, licking the butter from her lips once she was done. She peered into my eyes and the look on her face was one I was certainly familiar with. Really, nothing about Maria's outer appearance had aroused me until now, but I believe my vulnerability changed my perspective as if I was now peering at her through a different set of eyes.

She fed me another shrimp, then another and another one. Once I ate the last bite of the shrimp, she slid her index finger into my warm mouth and I clenched my lips around her small finger. She slowly removed her finger as we peered into each other's eyes. A wave of heat descended down to my clitoris, making it pulsate, and suddenly I became alert. The emotions Tobias stirred up inside of me vanished and at that moment, I simply wanted to pop this pussy for Maria.

She bent down and as she got closer, my lips began to tremble in excitement. I was eager to shove my tongue down her throat.

Beep! Beep!

Sir'Mahd

Enraged, I stormed down the hallway. I barged inside the bathroom, immediately spotting a dumbfounded King and Tonya. Tonya was still in the same position, only now she wasn't sucking dick. She was peering up at King, smiling as she used the cheap baby wipe to clean his dick.

Whack!

The impact from the strike forced Tonya's neck to snap before she fell on her ass. King eyed me in bewilderment.

"This the motherfucking thief right here! But you too blind to see that 'cause she sucking the life out your ass!"

King glared at her.

"Wait, wait! King," she begged, holding up her hands. "Sir! I didn't steal anything. What are you talking about?" she asked as the tears began to roll down her eyes.

"Bitch, don't question me. Just get the fuck out before I kill yo' ass. I fed you, bitch, put bread in your pockets, and you play me? You and ya clique. All three of you hoes done." I spoke in a low and serious tone.

113

She stood to her feet, using the back of her hand to remove the blood from her lip. She bypassed King and I with her head down .

"Aye!" I called out, making her turn around. "Where does Syren live?" I inquired.

"I don't——" Tonya started.

Whack!

"Lie again, bitch!" I yelled, hovering over Tonya's limp body. Yo' hating ass know where she stay. Don't be mad 'cause she taking your spot. You shouldn't've been stealing!" King hollered from a distance.

"Oh, she don't have to worry about that. Her spot is going to be taken, but not by Syren," I said, clearing things up. I had other plans for Syren. By now Tonya's eyes were swollen shut. I didn't give no fucks. I was about ready to break her nose.

"She stay in the motel next to the Chocolate City. I'm not sure which room number. You would have to just look for her car," she whispered in pain.

"And that is?"

"A late model black Honda Civic," she and King spoke in unison.

"Tell them other two hoes they fired too, and find two more. Three or four is too much. I'll get with you later. I got business to handle," I spoke quickly while jogging towards the rear of the house.

I had to find Syren and I had to find her now. Shorty had to really be down on her nuts, staying in a shitty room next to Chocolate City. I sped through the lights as if the cops were behind me. I couldn't begin to form in words exactly what and how I felt about this chick and why I was even feeling this way, but here I was.

Syren

I applied the last touches of makeup. I had locked up on a quick gig at the Chocolate City club next door. The owner who was trying to convince me to dance finally agreed to allow me to waitress on the day shift, since there were enough waiters at night. Popping

114

pussy at the low budget club would be a waste of time since most of the dancers sold pussy rather than throw ass.

I had been crying since yesterday. Symphony finally left my side an hour ago to go to work. I grabbed a Kleenex off the shelf to blot my eyes before walking out the door. Surprisingly, I spotted Sir'Mahd leaning against his G Wagon. He held the crotch of his jeans as he peered in my direction. I couldn't tell if he was looking into my eyes because the fitted he wore was pulled down extremely low.

"So you just gon' sell yourself short like that?" he asked in a low tone.

"Like what? And what is it to you anyways? You kicked me out your spot like I was a stray dog," I shot back, proceeding to my car.

"Aye," he uttered, stepping into my personal space and blocking the path to my car.

I smacked my lips as I stood there with my hand on my hip, peering up at him.

"I made a mistake, baby girl. I just want you to forgive me so I can make it up to you."

"You're forgiven. Now excuse me." I walked past him, slightly brushing against him before opening the door to my Honda.

"What time ya shift end?" he asked before climbing into his G Wagon.

"What? How you kn——"

"Come on, Syren, I'm a street nigga."

With that, he climbed inside his vehicle and drove off. Moments later, I did the exact same.

Later that night

I waved goodbye to the annoying old men that allowed me to make the same amount in one day as if I was still working at the spot. It was extremely difficult trying to focus on the task at hand when all I thought about was Sir'Mahd. Seeing him on the other side of my motel door was a scene I envisioned so many days ago since our first encounter. However, the day he badmouthed me and put me out broke my heart. His words stung. Perhaps I didn't expect it. I assumed he'd be lenient since we shared a connection, but I was wrong.

"I'll see you tomorrow. Same time, right?" the owner asked, blocking my path to the exit.

"Yeah, of course."

He politely slid to the side and I proceeded out of the club. I had heard horrible things about the small club. Shit, staying in the room these few weeks I'd heard gunshots. Today wasn't all that bad, but then again, this was the day shift.

"Shit! You scared me," I whispered loudly as soon as I spotted Sir'Mahd leaning against the hood of my car.

"I apologize, but now that your shift is over, can I take you out to eat?"

"No. I'm tired, Sir'Mahd. It's been a long day," I lied, attempting to fake a yawn.

"Well, that sucks I gue——"

"Ms. Syren!" Amyah jumped out of Sir'Mahd's truck and ran towards me yelling. She wrapped her tiny arms around my leg and squeezed me tight. I could felt her heart beating against my calf.

"Hey Amyah!" I bent down and hugged her back. It truly amazed me just how much she loved my presence.

She wrapped her arms around my neck. "I missed you, Ms. Syren! I have so much to tell you."

I peered up at Sir'Mahd and rolled my eyes before mouthing the words "slick ass" so Amyah couldn't hear me. He flashed his perfect smile while shrugging his shoulders.

"And sweetie, I can not wait to hear it."

"Come on, Ms. Syren, we have to hurry!"

"Okay, hunny, but I will have to meet up with y'all. I can't leave my car here."

"Yes you can. My daddy bought you a new one."

I looked from Amyah to Sir'Mahd, confused, unsure of what was occuring.

"What she talking about, Sir'Mahd?"

"His and her Wagons," he confirmed, holding up the keys.

116

I eyed the big Mercedes Benz symbol on the alarm device, my hands trembling in amazement and excitement.

"You want to freshen up before we go eat?" he asked.

"Definitely."

"Just leave that here," he said, referring to my car.

"That's fine, but I still owe the guy two hundred dollars."

"Oh, he'll never see that. That car should've been given away anyways. Let him pick it up and resell it."

When Sir'Mahd turned to walk away, I smiled. I loved that cocky shit.

I grabbed Amyah by the hand and the three of us climbed inside the truck. I could see the light pink G-Wagon as soon as we exited the lot of the club. The motel was literally next door. My smile widened as I peered at the truck in disbelief. He came to a stop in front of my room.

"I'll be right back. Wait, would you like to come inside?" Ashamed of the small space, I was hoping they would say no.

"Yeess!" Amyah chimed in.

"Come on, Amyah." I tilted my head towards my room while peering at Sir'Mahd.

Slowly he exited the vehicle. I believe he could sense how I felt. I opened the door to my room and immediately Amyah fell in love with the cheap vanity I had put together. She sat in the chair and began pulling out pallets of makeup.

"Leave her stuff alone, Amyah, and come sit down," Sir'Mahd stated.

"She's okay!" I yelled as I gathered my things to shower.

"Yeah, Dad, I want my makeup to be pretty like Ms. Syren's."

I chuckled at Amyah's comment before opening the door to the restroom. Out of the corner of my eye, I saw Sir'Mahd eyeing the pictures that were hung on my wall. He was so sexy. His face was faded and lined up to perfection. I just wanted to run my tongue across it. Realizing I was staring, I rushed inside the restroom and closed the door.

Tae

I had been sitting in the small dimly-lit room for what felt like days. My ass ached from sitting on the steel and I was in dire need of food and water. I wondered where Bunz was at. Hopefully she was somewhere in better conditions. Hopefully she wasn't telling these motherfuckers nothing.

The door to the room opened. I watched dude from the time he entered up until he took a seat. It was the same dude dressed in the "FEDS" shirt who cuffed us and led us to this place. I looked at him like he had shit on his face. I was beyond irritated. It was never part of the plan to leave us in here for so long.

"Change of plans, Bre'untae. Forgive me for taking so long. I've been next door talking to your…friend," he said, shooting me a questioning look.

"You right. Friend. We're just friends." My stomach turned as I thought about the conversation that might have transpired between the two. My thoughts became negative and instantly I became angry at Bunz. "So what's the new plan?" I asked, trying to appear unfazed.

"I want the both of you to help me take down Maine."

"And why the fuck would I help you pin charges on my brother?" I asked, insulted.

"Because you killed De'Kari. Bunz already cracked and admitted to shooting De'Kari. You can be charged for failure to render aid and spend up to ten years in prison," he informed me.

My mouth hit the floor. I shook my head from side to side in disbelief. I sighed deeply. " Can I talk to Bunz first?"

He flashed a boyish grin. "Sure. Five minutes is all you get."

Seconds later, he lightly shoved me inside the room with Bunz. Although I was deeply upset with her, I felt enthused to see her. She looked exhausted.

"Hey Bunz, I ca——"

"They're listening. Whatever you have to say, mouth it. I can read lips," she said, cutting me off.

Soundlessly, Bunz and I conversed back and forth.

118

"Did you agree to help them take down my brother?" I mouthed, peering at her, confused.

She returned the look of confusion. "Why the hell would I do that?"

"Well, since they know we killed De'Kari——"

"What?" Her eyes bucked in fear. She looked disheveled and stupefied.

"The dude told me you agreed to shooting De'Kari," I quickly admitted.

She rolled her eyes so hard you would've thought one was stuck. "And instead of cuffing us and pinning us with charges, he wanted us to help him take down Maine."

I nodded in agreement as Bunz lowered her head and smirked.

"Did you deny anything?"

"How could I when you had already tol——"

"You fell for the fucking okeydoke. You know why that nigga was in here for so long? 'Cause I wouldn't say shit. You did exactly what I told you *not* to do."

I lowered my head in defeat as I thought about how the white boy tricked me into incriminating myself and Bunz. However, I couldn't blame no one but me. Her nostrils flared so wide I just knew she was about to attack.

"Times up," the dude yelled as he opened the door.

"I'm going to get us out of this" I voiced loud enough for her and anyone else to hear.

"So what's it going to be?" he asked before we made it inside the other room.

"Whatever we got to do to stay free," I assured him. I felt so disgusted. Although Maine and I weren't as close as we used to be, he was still my brother.

"All I need is for you to sign on the dotted line and you're free to go"

"What about Bunz?" I inquired.

"She'll have to sign too."

"Okay." I nodded.

He left me standing in the dark hallway. He appeared a few minutes later with a few papers in his hand. My nerves were so bad I thought I was surely going to shit in my pants as I signed my name on the dotted line.

With just my phone and car keys ,I stood in the lot of the precinct waiting on Bunz. I had eight missed calls from Jaelyn, and the calls were seconds apart. Immediately, I phoned him back. It rang and rang, but no luck in reaching Jaelyn. I tried again.

I spotted Bunz walking towards me. Once I heard the answering machine, I ended the call.

"What took you so long?" I asked as soon as she got close enough.

"I was reading the paper I signed. Something you should've done. If you would've done what I told you to do, we wouldn't be signing shit!"

"Calm down, man," I tried reasoning.

"Nah, bruh, you're so contradicting and indecisive."

"The fuck you mean by that?"

"You murk a nigga for plotting to rob your brother, but then in black and white you agree to work with the pigs to put him behind bars for Lord knows how long."

"You're right. I'm not gon' let nobody fuck him over if I can stop it. But in this situation where it's him or me, I'm choosing my life, my freedom, for sho'."

"The bottom line, you can't be trusted, and after we do whatever it is they want us to do, I'm bouncing."

"Bitch, bye. You can bounce now if you want!" I shot back angrily.

"Nawl, I'm glued to ya hip now. I'on know what you'll try next. You might change ya mind and try to flee the country, and if you do, I'm gon' be right beside you. We'll both be living in a hut in Mexico."

"Look, Bunz, just for today can you stay in a room? I promise you we can link up tomorrow."

She stared at me for forever before saying, "You got twenty-four hours." She didn't utter anything else. She just headed into her own direction.

I sat at the bus stop to hitch a ride back to the room so I could get in my whip and check in with Iesha. I also made a mental note to see about Jaelyn.

***

"Oh my God! Tae, where have you been?" Iesha yelled as soon as I walked through the door of our cozy apartment.

"I got into a bit of jam, mama," I responded, unable to give her eye contact. I was so ashamed. I felt horrible for the pain I caused and the pain that was soon to come once I informed her about Bunz.

"What kind of jam that had you M.I.A. for two days?" she screamed while grabbing a hold of me. "Look at me!" she continued. She looked upset and exhausted. Her tears flowed without ceasing and at that moment, my heart ached for the woman I fell in love with so many years ago. I was a bit hesitant as I peered down into her eyes.

"Iesha, now you know me and De'Kari used to run together. Well, he got jammed up, and so did me and Bunz. We lost nearly everything we hit for and Bunz has nowhere to go, so she ——"

"Who is Bunz? Huh, Tae?"

"I just told you, Iesha," I said as I began to undress.

"Fuck it. I don't give a damn what you do as long as you're here and safe," she voiced squeezing me tightly. I wrapped my arms around her too and rocked from side to side enjoying the moment.

"Bae, let's lay down," I suggested. The bags under her eyes were proof she hadn't slept. Dressed in a size too big T-shirt, I led her to the bedroom. I admired her slim thick frame as she climbed onto our king-sized bed.

"Come lay with me, Tae."

"Let me shower real quick."

"Uh-uh, come on, please," she begged.

Dressed in nothing but a sports bra and briefs, I climbed into the bed with Iesha. I lay on my back, peering up at the ceiling while bae lay with her body stretched over mine and her head rested on my chest. Feeling the warm tears as they rolled down my abdominal section, I held Iesha tighter in an attempt to soothe her tears. My eyelids grew heavy as I continued to slowly run my hand up and down her spine. I wasn't sure if it was the lack of sleep or simply the comfort of my own home. I bent down and pecked a sleeping Iesha on the forehead. Poor woman must've cried herself to sleep. Fluffing the pillow underneath my head was the last thing I remember before falling into a deep slumber.

***

I jumped up at the sound of my phone ringing. I guess my sudden movement is what awoke bae as well.

"Who is it, bae?" she asked as I peered down at the screen.

Ignoring her question, my eyes bucked in fear instantly after spotting Bunz's name. " Hello?" I answered. I didn't know what to expect.

"Tae, it's some weird shit going on over here. I can't sleep. I'm afraid to move. It's uncomfortable and I'm exhausted. Come get me," she demanded. Her voice quivered a bit so I knew she was certainly afraid.

"I'm on my way. Send me the address."

"Okay."

Click!

"That was Bunz. Someone stalking her room trying to rob her," I quickly admitted.

"I'm coming with you," Iesha said, jumping to her feet.

"Come on."

Syren

The past few days I had been feeling like shit. Yesterday I went to a nearby clinic for pregnancy and COVID testing. I found out an hour ago I tested negative for both. I knew I was negative. Getting tested was merely proper procedure. Something else was wrong, but I couldn't detect it. There was this vile feeling in the pit of my stomach that I just couldn't shake. I had two anxiety attacks in the past three days which left me no choice but to go to the hospital. Jaelyn had been on my mind and heart heavy, but my mother was too, which I didn't find odd because every time I was away from them, I missed and thought of them often.

After going out to eat with Amyah and Sir'Mahd, he convinced me to stay the night. Since I didn't felt too good, he was better than any doctor I've had. He catered to every need and he was very attentive.

We didn't sleep until the rays of sun began to peek through the blinds. The entire night we shared goals, upbringings, fears, dreams, etc. Sir'Mahd was exactly how I thought he was - a tough guy on the outside, but inwardly he wanted to love and be loved. He just refused to give his heart to anyone. He possessed all the traits of a good dude but, at the same time he was zero-tolerant to things that weren't beneficial, productive or essential to him. I actually regret leaving so soon but, then again I didn't want to wear out my welcome. Tears fell from my eyes and down my cheeks I was an emotional mess and truthfully, I had no idea why. The same shirt that adorned my body, I used it as tissue to dry my tears.

Knock! Knock! Knock!

I looked towards the door, confused. I hadn't heard from Symphony in two days. Maybe it was her.

"I brought brunch," Sir'Mahd said, holding the Chipotle bag up.

I was ecstatic to see his handsome face and my smile was indeed proof. "I'm so glad to see you, Sir'Mahd." My eyes lit up like a kid's on Christmas day.

"Yeah, I hear you. I just saw that nigga leave ten minutes ago," he said, putting the bag down on the table.

"Boy, quit lying!" I yelled, playfully punching him in the arm. "Mmm, that smells good, Sir'Mahd," I said as soon as he opened the container and handed me my food. "Wait, you already ate?"

"Yeah, I grabbed some tenders from Grandy's about an hour ago.

"Oooh, I love Grandy's! Where is Amyah?"

"Piano lessons. She told me to give you this," he said before leaning in and kissing me on the lips.

He pulled away before I could even react. His lips felt softer than they looked, the sweet gesture really caught me by surprise.

"Oh. Well, what do you have for me?" I asked seductively.

"What I brought," he responded without looking my way.

"Oh, I see you got jokes. That's cool. Keep that same energy," I joked, chewing my food. I stretched my legs out, placing them directly into his lap. "Can you rub my feet?"

"You shower yet? 'Cause I'm not trying to have that scent on my hands."

"Boy! You play too damn much!" I chuckled while eyeing my phone.

Ring! Ring! Ring!

The number was unfamiliar, but I answered anyway.

"Hello?"

"Momma?"

"Jaelyn! Hello?"

"Momma, it's me. Can you come get me?"

Jaelyn

I awoke curled up in the same small space I'd been in for the past few days. I was uncertain of the amount of days. I just knew it felt like forever since the night I returned home from Monty's. The man I admired and worshipped all my life had beat me like I was a guy on the streets. There weren't a lot of words exchanged, but I do know he found out about the male-on-male pornography I'd been watching. The pornography had been a guilty pleasure that I kept hidden from everyone besides Monty. I still couldn't believe I was so sloppy. How could I forget to delete it?

"Aagghh." I winced at the sudden pain shooting up my side. I gripped my side tight to subside the pain. The horrible smell made me queasy. I was afraid to turn and stretch my legs because I'd pissed on myself twice and vomit lay on both sides of me. I was so hungry my head ached. It felt like my temples were about to bust. Tears streamed down my face rapidly. I hated Maine. I hated his beliefs, morals, and values. I hated who he was, and the man he'd become. He was a judgmental, biased, evil sack of shit, and when the opportunity presented itself, I was going to kill him and spit on his casket at the funeral.

I used my forearm to remove the tears from my face. I knew it was swollen because the warm liquid burned whatever cut or scars I had. For a long time he led me to believe that I couldn't love both parents equally due to their beliefs. At the time I didn't understand, even when he defined the terms " beliefs". I guess I was just too young to grasp it. The only thing I knew was that I wanted to be just like Maine. I wanted him to be proud of me and admire me just as I did him, even if it meant emotionally harming my mother in the process. There was no way my mother would've ever done something so mean and sadistic.

I could feel myself going in and out of consciousness. I hoped soon Maine would at least have the heart to come check on me because I was unsure of how much longer I could hold on.

***

"Jaelyn! Jaelyn!"

Through squinted eyes I peered at Maine, who stood over me. The bright light was pestering me as I held up my arm weakly to block it out.

"Huh?" I answered weakly. If I had an ounce of strength I'd rush his ass, but being deprived of food, water, and sunlight for days really took a toll on me.

"Go get yourself cleaned up so you can eat," he demanded, watching me like an animal in a cage.

I leaned up. I guess I moved too quickly because instantly I became dizzy. I leaned against the wall for leverage.

"Come on!" he snapped. I tried again, gripping the si

de of the wall to pull myself up. It was extremely painful, but I did it.

Maine peered at me in disgust. I reeked of vomit and piss and now that I was standing just a few feet away, he really caught a whiff. "The fuck you walking so slow?"

I didn't even bother to respond. I limped towards the restroom, using the wall for support. I entered the restroom, immediately spotting the empty tub. Lord knows I wasn't going to be able to stand long enough to take a shower. I didn't bother to ask why the tub wasn't filled. I was tired of his inconsiderate remarks. I crouched down and turned the knob on the hot water and watched the water slowly fill the tub. I peered into the large mirror and tears began to burn my sockets, blurring my vision, but I refused to give this nigga something to talk about. He didn't know, but he was dead to me. I untied and removed my sneakers, then unzipped my jeans. "You going to stand there?" I asked, looking back at him annoyed.

"Yeah. You got a problem with that? You like watching other niggas, you faggot. What's wrong with me watching you?"

Treated like a prisoner in my own home. I tried to appear unfazed by the harsh words that undeniably bruised my ego. Although I felt weak, I moved as fast as I could so he wouldn't lash out and hit me again. Between the knots, bruises, and gash I already had, I couldn't afford any more. I stepped in the tub and the moment my ass connected with the bottom, I felt like I was in heaven.

Suddenly, his phone rang and he put it on speakerphone "Hello?"

"Bossman, the laws up here looking for you?"

"For what?"

"They're investigating a murder."

"A murder? The fuck! I'm on my way!" he yelled, running out of the restroom.

As soon as I heard the front door close, I squirted the Irish Spring body wash on the towel and scrubbed my body as if I was being timed. The burst of energy came out of the blue. I hit the important spots, rinsed the soap off of me, and hopped out. Snatching the towel off the rack, I patted my body dry. I couldn't apply too much pressure. I was already in pain. I ran across the hall to my room and retrieved a pair of briefs. I scanned around quickly for my phone, but it was nowhere in sight. Neither was the laptop or tablet. My shoulders sagged in defeat. I had to contact Monty.

"Monty!" I voiced aloud as I thought about the tablet his mother purchased both of us last Christmas that I kept underneath my bed. I retrieved the Burberry shoebox from underneath my bed and removed the $280 I had saved up and the tablet. I quickly powered on the tablet and instantly, messages from my message app surfaced. There were multiple messages from Monty. I didn't bother to contact Tae. I had called Monty several times the night it all happened, right before Maine burst in and confiscated everything.

"I'm on my way," I texted, sliding the tablet into my book bag. I quickly got dressed and threw my bookbag over my shoulder. I rummaged through the fridge, devouring a few snacks.

Bing!

"Okay. Where have you been? I been worried sick!"

"Send an Uber my way, I have the money," I replied. A minute or so later I received a text from Monty assuring me that the Uber was en route. I thought I was going to shit on myself as I stood in the living room drinking a Gatorade while peering out the blinds, awaiting the arrival of the Uber driver. I rushed to the back and inside of my room to fill my bookbag with essentials because for certain I wasn't going to return.

A car horn sounded from outside.

"Shit!" I yelled, nearly falling. I tripped over the corner of the bed as I bolted out of the room then out the door. I shut the front door behind me and hopped inside the Chevy Malibu.

"How are you?" the beautiful mixed breed chick asked.

"I'm good." I reclined into the seat and listened to the Summer Walker lyrics that played at a moderate volume.

Twenty minutes later, we pulled up and I got out of the Uber.

"Jaelyn!" Monty rushed outside and hugged me as soon as I stepped out of the backseat.

I hugged him back, although it was painful. I missed him. Visions of Maine kicking me in my ribs surfaced in the midst of Monty and me hugging, causing me to quickly let go.

"What's wrong?" Monty asked, confused.

"Look, I need to use your phone. I'm about to call my mother."

Uh'Nija

"Shit!" Maria yelled, jumping to her feet.

Tobias's return made me a bit uneasy as well, but I still wanted my kiss. I quickly hopped to my feet as she gathered the utensils.

"Maria," I whispered, just inches away from her face.

"Huh?" she responded, facing me.

I leaned in, pressing my lips into hers. They weren't as soft, but they were big, just how I liked them. "We'll finish up another time." I pulled back and sat on the bed and finished off my food.

My phone rang. "Hello?" I answered

"Ms. Marshall, this is Dr. Debois from the women's clinic. I have both good and bad news that I'll prefer to give to you in person. Can we set an appointment? What's the earliest time you can come by in the morning?"

"Uh…what's the earliest you have available?"

"Ten."

"Okay. I'll be there."

"See you then, Ms. Marshall."

My heartbeat sped up. I didn't know what could've possibly transpired. I was scheduled to receive my COVID results yesterday, but I unwittingly forgot about it after hearing the news regarding the pregnancy.

"Fuck!" I should've made him tell me whatever it is over the phone because the idea of not knowing was going to have me on edge. I decided I wasn't going to tell Tobias until after I found out what was going on.

He and Maria appeared to be in a deep conversation when I walked up.

"Yes, Uh'Nija," Tobias said before I could even speak. He seemed a little frustrated, but he quickly hid it well.

I inched closer and said, "I'm going to bed early 'cause I have an interview with the administration counselor at Ogle's cosmetology school."

"But you already know how to do hair."

"Yes, I do, but there are other fundamentals I have yet to grasp. Mani, pedis, facials, and whatever else. You take damn good care of me. The least I can do is properly utilize my time and make something of myself so I can one day take care of you too," I exaggerated.

Tobias pulled me closer by my waist and gently kissed me on the lips. "That's fine with me," he agreed.

Indeed, I was going to take a trip to the nearest Ogle, but I had no real intentions on actually attending school. But just in case he wanted to check my trap, I had to keep my word.

I took a shower, then climbed in bed. I used the towel to dry my hair, making my bundles look extremely curly after removing the towel. I scrolled down the news feed on my Instagram until I drifted off to sleep.

I awoke the next morning feeling rejuvenated. Tobias woke me up in the middle of the night to the best pipe that's ever been laid. He kissed me on the forehead before leaving about an hour or so prior to me waking up. I lightly beat my face and straightened my hair before leaving the house. My nerves were shot the entire ride to the clinic. I kept telling myself to think positive, but it was hard to do when the doctor said that there was good news and bad. I parked in the nearest empty spot and rushed inside.

"Hi, I'm Uh'Nija Marshall. I have a ten o'clock appointment with Dr. Debois." I spoke so fast that I stammered over my words.

"Okay, wait right there and he'll be with you in a sec," the stringy-haired clerk informed me.

I took a seat in the lobby as instructed as I listened to a Dr. Oz podcast.

"Ms. Marshall!"

I bolted out my seat like fire was under my feet as I raced towards his office. Shutting the door behind me, I flopped down onto the seat.

"How you doing, Ms. Marshall?"

"I'm fine, Doc. If you don't mind, I'd like it if you'd just cut to the chase."

"Sure, no problem. Ms. Marshall, there seems to have been a huge mix up and first and foremost, I truly apologize."

"Mix up?"

"Yes. You're not pregnant. Your urine was mistaken for someone else's."

"I guess that's the good news?" The news was stunning, but relieving at the same time. There's no way I would've been able to live with myself knowing that I aborted my baby. "Okay, and the bad news is?"

"You tested positive for Herpes Simplex B."

"What?"

"Calm down, Ms. Marshall," he voiced calmly.

"Hell nah, herpes? What is B?"

"Well, Simplex A is when the sores break out on your mouth. Simplex B is when the sores break out on or inside your vagina."

"Lord, I can't believe this shit right here," I said as tears fell from my eyes. Herpes is just fucked up because there's not a cure for it.

"Truthfully, I thought you'd be glad to find out you're not actually pregnant."

"How will I know when I've had an outbreak?"

"Ms. Marshall, you'll definitely feel it. Depending on where the sore is located determines the pain. It can be inside like it was recently, making it difficult for you to urinate. I've heard the ones outside of your urethra can be painful simply from walking."

I covered my face with both palms.

"I'm going to prescribe you some pills that will decrease your outbreaks and subdue the pain whenever you have an outbreak," he said, handing me the result paper.

"You know, Doc, I had no clue I was going to be hit with the herpes bomb."

"Ms. Marshall, another thing. Whenever you do have an outbreak, herpes can be transmitted. If I were you, I'd inform my partner, keep my partners at a minimum and go on as if it's not there. Take your pills once a day and you'll be fine." Doctors were so kind and patient.

"Thank you for everything, Dr. Debois," I said, standing to my feet.

I stopped by the pharmacy counter on my way out to retrieve my medicine. The disturbing news had drained me mentally and physically. I didn't even want to stop by the school anymore. The ride home I wondered which man had given me the incurable disease. I was so tired of selling myself short. Deep down I truly believed Tobias had given me this disease, and after witnessing the shit a few nights ago, I knew I didn't love him like my mind led me to believe.

Gratefully, he hadn't made it home he was still out and about. I spotted Maria as soon as I stepped inside.

"Hey girl," she greeted, kissing me on the lips.

"Heeey, I'm drained, Maria. That school was big as shit."

"Come lie down so I can rub your feet," she urged, grabbing me by the hand.

"Nah, Maria, I don't feel like getting up."

"Okay." She knelt down, removing my sandals. She went to retrieve lotion and returned immediately. She massaged my heel and in between my toes. The sensation was so relaxing I closed my eyes. Her hands began to move upward. She caressed my calves, knees, then my thighs. I peered down at her when she began to lift my sundress.

"Lay back," she whispered.

I smiled deviously and let her do her thing.

She lifted my dress and I could tell by the way she paused that me not wearing any underwear caught her by surprise.

"Hold them," she demanded, pinning my legs up.

The position resembled one of a woman giving birth. I held onto my knees while Maria went to work. Gently she rubbed her tongue up and down my opening licking and slurping on my lips. Suddenly she attacked my clit. Her tongue moved quickly from left to right on my love button. I started thrusting forward. She paused before carefully slurping it with abnormal speed. She flicked her tongue across my clit again. I hadn't had top like this in a long time. I let go of one of my legs and grabbed her by the hair. She sucked and slurped as I continued to thrust.

"Fuck yeah!" I hollered, biting my lip to control another outburst. The pace of my thrusts quickened. I used my two fingers to pull back the skin that surrounded my love button, which intensified the feeling. My head fell back onto the couch. This shit was better than amazing. "Im cumming!" I yelled as my legs quivered. She sped up and I exploded, gripping her head with my thighs. Once the last drip of honey fell, I loosened my grip and my feet hit the floor weakly.

"Can you make me something to eat? I'm going to shower as soon as I regain my strength." I was dead ass.

A few hours later, I sat up in the cozy king-sized bed, scrolling down the tablet at the apartment listings, when Tobias walked in.

"Hey love," he greeted

"Hey boo. I missed your face. What's that you got there?" I asked, pointing at the little pink box.

"You so damn nosy," he said, putting it behind his back .

"Give it to me. Don't be like that." I jumped out of bed and leaped on him, wrapping my long legs around his waist.

"Whoa! I'm going to give you something, but it's not going to be this box," he joked, wrapping his arms around me.

I lay my head on his shoulder enjoying the alluring and masculine scent that mesmerized me months ago when we first met. "Make love to me, Tobias," I whispered into his ear before slowly tracing the edge of it with my tongue.

He threw me on the bed, placed the box on the dresser and slowly peeled off his clothes. I lay on my back, leaning on my elbows as I watched him unblinkingly. Dressed in one of his old Tshirts with no undergarments on, I placed my hand in my pool of wetness, slurping it off my finger. Tobias placed the little pink box on his thick log, which stood at attention.

"Come get it," he teased.

I crawled to the edge of the bed then reached out and grabbed the box. The twenty-four carat yellow diamond tennis bracelet lit up like the sky on the Fourth of July. It was breathtaking.

"Aww, thank you, baby," I said before spreading my legs. I lifted the shirt over my head and tossed it on the floor exposing my pecan-colored breasts.

Tobias grabbed me by the thighs, pulling me nearly off the bed, his nine inch penis tapping my opening. He peered deeply into my eyes as he inched deeper inside of my sanctuary. I clawed at his hands that gripped my legs while biting my lip.

"Oooh shit!"

His strokes were deep and sweet, slow and measured. He was giving me exactly what I asked for. With one hand he pulled me closer by my slim waist, and with the other, he rubbed my love button.

"Turn around."

Slowly but surely I did so, tooting my ass in the air. He gripped my ass cheeks spreading them before falling inside of my wetness. The herpes sore inside of my pussy itched and every stroke he scratched it. His pace sped up and the weaker I became, yet I never stopped throwing this ass back.

"I'm cumming, daddy!" I yelped out in pleasure.

"Me too!" he muttered. Moans and grunts filled the room.

"Daddy!" I hollered as the sweet cream departed from the jar.

"Aarrghhh!" Tobias roared merely seconds later. He collapsed on top of me and we remained in that position, breathing heavily.

I awoke what seemed to be hours later. The sun was no longer out, and there was no noise of any form coming from outside. If I was going to move, it was going to have to be now. I was done with staying with someone to keep them happy even when I wasn't.

I used to think Tobias was too good for someone like me. Growing up in dysfunction and being in dysfunctional relationships all my life was what I was accustomed to and was obviously what I wanted and desired because I was bored with Tobias. I felt as if he was a good man who deserved a good woman, but after witnessing him and this conniving bitch who portrayed to be just his maid going at it like newlyweds I was disgusted. He was just like Maine's dirty dick ass and the rest of them. I knew I didn't love him like I thought because with my attitude, I would've killed him and that bitch in the midst of their sex session. Instead, I had turned and walked away, returned to the bedroom, and started plotting. Finding out about the incurable disease was truly a bummer, but I'd be able to penalize those who harmed me in the process.

Quickly and quietly, I stuffed clothes and shoes inside the Dior luggage. All the jewelry and miscellaneous items I adored, I placed them inside my purse. I used the back of an old receipt and a marker and wrote:

Tobias and Maria I hope the two of you enjoy your lives. I left something with the both of you for the rest of your lives.
Uh'Nija

I took one last glance around the room and even Tobias's sexy ass before I closed the door and that chapter of my life.

Tae

"Come outside. I'm here," I spoke into the phone as Iesha and I waited outside her room.

Bunz strutted out of the room, appearing unfazed by the activity she assumed was going on outside her room. Oddly, things were quiet, but nothing appeared out of the ordinary. I cut my eyes at Iesha and sure enough, her lips were poked out.

"Hmph," she sounded.

I sighed, knowing the reason behind the smirk on her face.

Bunz made her way to my car looking edible. The Express joggers and crop top hugged her body like a latex glove. The forty inch bundles bounced with each step. Her hair almost touched the top of her cream-colored knee high boots. The site of Bunz made my mouth water, but I could tell she made Iesha's blood boil. She peered at me as if an unfamiliar and strong offensive odor filled the car and I was the cause of it.

What?" I asked, pretending to appear dumbfounded.

"Shut up. Just leave me alone," Iesha warned.

"What's - my bad," Bunz said, opening the passenger door but quickly retreating to the backseat once realizing the seat was already taken. "Hey y'all," she continued once she was seated in the back.

"What's up, B?" I spoke.

Iesha said, "Hey," but it was dry as hell.

Bunz and I made eye contact for a split second through the rearview mirror the smirk plastered on her face instantly gave me an eerie feeling. Before things became extremely awkward, I focused on the road ahead and increased the volume of the music. I was unsure why I dreaded going inside my own home, but sadly, I did. I killed the engine and the three of us climbed out.

"Tae, can you grab the other suitcase for me?" she asked.

I peered at Iesha. She pinched the bridge of her nose and proceeded upstairs. "Yeah, hold on." The leather suitcase was light as a feather. I stopped and peered directly in front of her through narrow slits.

"What?"

"Bunz, what the fuck, man?" I spoke through clenched teeth.

"Well, I got a bit nervous. Too many hours had passed since I heard from you."

"Yeah but we——"

"Fuck an agreement," she cut in, raising her voice a bit.

I peered around. Iesha stood at the rail in front of our apartment door, looking down at us.

"Whatever, man," I mumbled, leading the way. The last thing I wanted was to make Iesha feel some type of way.

Once inside I placed Bunz's suitcase by the door and sprinted to our bedroom. Iesha was undressing. I could hear the water from the shower running.

"Mama, can I join you?"

"Of course, Tae," she responded.

I quickly peeled off the Air Max.

"Tae!" Bunz yelled.

"What's up?" I yelled from the doorway of my room.

"Where do I put my things?"

"Come here," I called out. "Put them in this closet," I said, pointing to the walk-in closet to the left.

"Okay, thanks."

I didn't even respond. I simply shut the door and joined Iesha.

Syren

"What a surprise! Of course I can come get you, baby."

"Okay. I'm about to text you the address."

"Okay. I'll see you then."

Click!

"Oh my God, Sir'Mahd, it was my son. Come on. We have to go get him," I voiced, full of excitement.

"Is he okay?" Sir'Mahd asked, a bit startled.

"Yes. I'm so excited because I haven't gotten a chance to spend time with him since I've been home," I explained.

"Oh, okay," he spoke slowly. I could tell by the wrinkles in his forehead he still didn't grasp it.

"Come on. I'll tell you all about it on our way."

"Bet."

By the time Sir'Mahd veered onto the unfamiliar street, I had informed him of a cluster of things, like the reason I was no longer with Maine, my mother being in the nursing home, why Maine didn't want me to have Jaelyn, and the reason Maine was so upset. He didn't judge. He simply listened and asked questions of his own. I had no problem giving him an answer. I told him everything so that no one else could if things between him and I went any further.

He pulled alongside the curb of the house he'd given me the address to. After several minutes of waiting, Jaelyn was still nowhere to be found. I tapped the screen, clicking on the last call I received, and called the number back.

"Hello?"

"Jaelyn, I'm outside," I announced, peering up the driveway.

Two boys bent the corner. I smiled once I realized it was Monty. Monty and Jaelyn were good friends before I did the two year bid and I was ecstatic to see they were still close. Wrinkles formed across my forehead the closer Jaelyn got.

"What's wrong with li'l man?" Sir'Mahd asked before I could utter a word.

"That's what the hell I'm trying to figure out," I responded, unbuckling my seatbelt and hopping out of the truck. My knees buckled as soon as I walked around the truck and came face to face with my son.

"Momma!" Jaelyn called out as he reached out in an attempt to break my fall.

"What happened? Who did this to you?" I shrieked as tears fell from my eyes. My heart raced like I just did a full cardio workout. I searched his eyes for answers, but I didn't find any. He appeared mortified and burdened. The sight of him made my heart shatter like glass and my entire body began to tremble as if I had Parkinson's. "Jaelyn! Do you hear me?" I asked, gripping the sleeves on his shirt. I could feel Sir'Mahd large hands caressing my shoulder.

"Monty, did you do this?"

"No ma'am," he replied, shaking his head swiftly.

"Baby, who did this to you?" I pried, pretending to be calm. My heart ached even more as I gazed at the damage that was done. I could tell by the crust and dried-up blood around the gash under his eye that whatever took place happened a little time ago. The knot a few inches above his brow was hardly noticeable, but the one in the middle of his forehead stuck out like a full moon.

"Come on, mama, he might not want to talk here and now. Let's go someplace comfortable." Sir'Mahd suggested.

I rose up, taking Jaelyn's hand into mine and we climbed into the backseat of Sir'Mahd's truck.

I knew something life-changing had occurred because once inside the truck, I scooted as close as possible to Jaelyn, draping my arm over his shoulder. From time to time I'd kiss the top of his head, but I didn't press him any more for answers.

Minutes later, we veered into Sir'Mahd's driveway and climbed out.

"Where's Amyah?" I asked.

"Her best friend's grandmother drops her off after ballet practice," he answered, opening the front door to his massive home.

I peered back at Jaelyn as he climbed the steps. He clutched his side as he winced in pain. "Do your ribs hurt too?"

He hesitated to respond, but when he did, it was simply, "Yes, ma'am."

"Come on," I said, grabbing him by the hand. Hand in hand, Jaelyn and I walked inside.

"There's a guest room to the left of Amyah's," Sir'Mahd whispered.

"Okay." I remembered my way around the house because I dreamed I was in it so many nights.

The tears blurred my vision as we walked down the long hallway I felt like a failure. I failed at something I could've so easily been successful at but, being that I put myself before my child I allowed my actions to hinder me from succeeding.

"Get comfortable," I told Jaelyn before walking towards the living room where Sir'Mahd was. "Do you mind if I make him a few snacks?" I asked Sir'Mahd.

"I brought you here to share this with you. This is not just my shit. It's our shit. We a family, Syren. Me, you, Amyah, and Jaelyn. Do whatever you want to do. You need me to do something?"

"No, I'm fine. Thank you for everything," I said before heading for the kitchen.

The fridge was full of groceries. I grabbed a variety of fruits and made him a fresh sandwich with wheat bread, lettuce, tomatoes, honey ham, and swiss cheese. I needed Jaelyn to remove his shirt so that I could see if his ribs were bruised. I entered the room with his drink and foods. Luckily his shirt had already been removed. I set everything next to him on the night stand as I examined his

138

midsection. Indeed, his ribs were bruised. I deeply sighed, unsure of what to do.

"You need this?" Sir'Mahd asked, standing in the doorway with the Ace bandage wrap in his hand.

"Yes," I agreed once I spotted it in his hand.

"Hey, li'l man, if you want I got the PS5 down there in my man cave whenever you want to play."

"Thanks, but I'm alright for now," Jaelyn responded in a low tone.

"I'll be back. Give you two some time alone." Sir'Mahd walked out, closing the door behind him.

"Did your dad do this to you?" I inquired as soon as the door closed.

"No."

"Well who did this to you?"

"I don't want to talk about it."

"Let me at least wrap you up."

Without any form of resisting he stood up and held his arms up. I moved quickly as I wrapped the stretchy material around his body. He reclined against the pillows, eating fresh grapes out of the small bowl as he peered around at the cultural black paintings that decorated the room. I grabbed the remote off the dresser and turned on the forty-six inch plasma that set in the center of the wall.

There was a knock on the door,

"Come in," I said.

"Hey, Ms. Syren!" Amyah yelled as soon as the door swung open.

"Jaelyn, this is Amyah. Amyah, this is Jaelyn."

Tae

It had been a total nightmare since the night Iesha and I picked Bunz up. Our one bedroom apartment wasn't much, but it was ours Lately, things had become intolerable and disheartening. Iesha nagged and harassed me as if I had been a cheater and liar our entire relationship. I couldn't shit, shower, or shave in peace. Iesha had never acted so insecure. Indeed, Bunz was a beautiful woman, but I was a woman with self-control. There were many beautiful women in the world. I couldn't sex them all. The majority of the time Iesha was trippin', but a time or two Bunz purposely said or did something that annoyed Iesha.

I'd been phoning Jaelyn for the past few days, but receiving no response. I was starting to think Maine took him with him to a foreign country so De'Kari wouldn't have a chance at getting him back. Little did Maine know De'Kari was dead. Although many scenarios ran through my mind, it wasn't enough for me to believe any of the assumptions. I still took it upon myself to pay Monty a visit a few days ago, but I was not ready for his response. He informed me that Syren was the one who had come to get him. It bothered me that I wasn't there to answer his call. Something had to have taken place for him to call Syren. Although Syren was his mother, hers and Jaelyn's relationship was a bit odd, if you ask me. I had tried calling Maine several times, but his phone was going straight to voicemail. I needed answers - now.

The cool breeze was refreshing as I leaned on the rail at the top of the stairs, peering down at the scenery below. Lately this was the best place to be because if I was anywhere inside of our small apartment out of Bunz's eyesight, she would be accusing me of any and everything.

My life had changed drastically. I hated both awkward positions I was in. Agreeing to be a snitch just so I wouldn't have to suffer the consequences for my actions, then the adversity I was causing in my own home.

"Come here, Tae," Iesha demanded.

I could tell by her facial expression that she was upset about something. I sighed deeply while headed in her direction.

"Did you tell her she can use the hallway closet as her storage?" she said loudly before the front door was even shut.

"Temporarily, yes," I said, frustrated.

"I told you, Iesha," Bunz boasted, coming from the restroom. Her clothes were revealing and provocative. The sheer crop top hugged her breasts, which were protruding like mini melons. You

140

could see her bare skin through the sheer leggings. She wore a G-string the same color of the leggings covering her plump box. Bunz looked enticing and Iesha must've sensed I felt that way.

"You can't sit around dressed like that," Iesha voiced.

"I know, I'm about to go. Damn, why you sweating me?"

"Good. You should've been gone."

"Hey Tae, can you take me downtown to the Omni hotel?" Bunz asked, completely ignoring Iesha.

"Bitch, my nigga not taking you nowhere dressed like that!"

"Who you calling a bitch first——"

"Chill!" I yelled, grabbing Iesha and dragging her to the bedroom. "What's wrong with you?" I asked, shutting the door behind me.

"Me? It's that bitch! I just don't understand this shit. It's dumb, bruh. She don't have no family? No nigga? Y'all hit all those licks. You got money saved up. Where her bread at? Why does she have to stay here?" she asked, teary-eyed.

I hated I didn't have a definite answer nor did I have any way of fixing the problem. There was no way I could simply say, "Hey, we killed someone, but neither one of us trusts one another, so we rather live under the same roof to watch each other's moves."

"Like I've told you a hundred times before she don't have anything. Just give it a few more months and I pro——"

"Months? Are you serious? I got one even better. Fuck you and her. I'm gone," she stated, moving around the room swiftly.

"Why? For what? Come on, Iesha, you gon' do me like this? Shit just fucked up right now. You gon' just leave?" I argued, completely stunned by her statement.

"Call me when shit is no longer fucked up, Bre'untae. I shouldn't have to live like this in my own home," Iesha declared while constantly packing her things.

The idea of Iesha leaving had crossed my mind a time or two but I overlooked it due to our bond and the love we have for one another. She showed me where I was wrong. My heart ached in the worst way watching the woman I loved walk out of my life. It felt as if my world was tumbling down and dismantling before my eyes.

I had to stop her. Something in my mental was telling me I couldn't live without her. I ran towards Iesha and grabbed her so that she couldn't escape my grip.

"Get off of me Tae!" she cried, trying to jerk away.

"No, Iesha. I love you. We can work this out. Don't do this shit! What you want from me?" Distress was plastered all over my face. I was hopeless. Tears cascaded down my face as I lay my head on her shoulder without releasing my death grip.

"I don't want to hear any excuses. Make her leave, Tae," she ordered.

Bunz leaving would mean putting my freedom on the line, spending the rest of my life behind bars. Bunz staying meant losing my soulmate, which would change my life drastically as well. Slowly, I released my grip and eased away from Iesha.

"Really? That bitch means that much to you?" she asked, startled by my indecision as she continued to peer at me dumbfounded through squinted eyes.

"It's not that. It's just I have to keep a close eye on her 'cause some gangsta shit went down," I whispered.

"Like what?" she asked in disbelief.

"I can't tell you that, mama. Just trust me," I begged, grabbing hold of her hand.

"Fuck you." She yanked away, leaving with the bags she had packed, and walking away.

***

"We already breaking the code. I just hope it's not any fuck shit involved," Bunz expressed.

Although I heard her, it was faintly. My mind was on Iesha and had been there these past few days since she vanished. Her presence had given me everything and when she left, she stripped me, leaving me with nothing but a broken heart.

Bunz and I were on our way to meet up with Doug, the ATF agent that wanted Maine.

"Tae? Tae?"

"Huh? What's up?" I asked, pretending to be attentive.

"You been tripping ever since ya li'l hoe left."

"Watch yo' mouth! She aint no hoe!" I snapped.

"You want some pussy? I got you. My shit A-1 since day one," she joked.

I didn't find shit funny. "Leave me alone, Bunz," I said, pulling into the lot.

Doug walked to my car and slid in, clutching a manilla envelope. "Here's the deal. I need you to get Maine to sell you a nice amount of product that'll put this motherfucker away for a long time, maybe forever."

Hearing the pig speak so harshly about Maine pierced my soul making me instantly regret the agreement I made. "Why so much?" I asked rhetorically.

"It's like this. I want a life for a life. You took someone's life. I'm going to spare yours only if I'm able to get a life in return. So look, I have fifty grand on me. It's the money you'll use to cop an adequate amount of methamphetamine."

"Methamphetamine?" I asked with a perplexed look on my face. "He don't fuck with that," I continued.

"Yeah, I know that, but I also know ya boy is greedy, and once he catches wind that you're willing to purchase the drugs gram for gram, he'll jump on the lick. Isn't that what you all call it?" he asked sarcastically.

"You funny," was all I said before Doug laid out a scandalous and well thought out plan on exactly how he wanted Bunz and I to take out Maine.

***

I found it quite odd that Maine asked me to meet him at Sandsprings park. The small park was in the middle of a section of residential homes that occupied at least two acres of land. Just a merry-go-round and a few seesaws that he and I played on as adolescents. Earlier that day I called him inquiring about Jaelyn's whereabouts, but right before the call ended, I told him I wanted to discuss business. I just knew he was going to reject the request, but to my surprise, he didn't. Something about his speech led me to believe Maine was troubled by something. To say afraid, I'd be exaggerating, but I did sense something to that degree.

I left Bunz back at the apartment while I handled things with Maine. It was a struggle convincing her to stay, but she did.

Peering through the rearview mirror, I spotted his car pull up directly behind mine. After a minute or so passed, I pulled out my phone to call him, but quickly put it away when I saw his car door open. I inhaled deeply then exhaled before Maine climbed inside. My hands were now trembling. I was that nervous.

"What's up?" he asked.

"Cooling. Trying to figure out what's up with you."

Maine sighed in exasperation. "Bruh, I don't know what the fuck I've gotten myself into. I can't and haven't talked to nobody 'cause I don't trust nobody, but all this shit on my chest is killing me."

"What's going on? Whatever it is, it sounds deep. How deep is this shit?" I asked concerned.

"They trying to pin a body on me. I'm not trying to see no prison walls. That shit lame, especially behind some shit I didn't do. I got a mama I got to see about. What about my seed?"

I peered at Maine as I thought, *Little do you know I'm the very one plotting to put you behind those same bars you detest so much.* I peered straight ahead, unable to look him in his eyes.

"They pop up at my place of employment demanding shit I don't have the answers to and threatening me with 50 years to life. I can't even count that fucking high."

"Fam, if you didn't do it, they can't pin it on you. I know you done copped the best attorney," I assured, looking at him.

"I did yesterday."

"So leave it alone. Let me rap with you about this cash flow," I said, trying to change the subject before he made me feel worse than what I was feeling.

"Shoot."

"This white boy I fuck with going out of town, him and some friends. They trying to get some meth. I already told them that shit federal and too many people don't fuck with it, so if I get ahold of some, they'll have to buy it regular price, gram for gram. They trying to spend fifty G's. So if you got a little plug on it, you'll win big time," I attempted to convince him.

"Hell yeah! I'll have that by tomorrow. That's just what I need. Just in case anything happens to me, I have to make sure Jaelyn and Momma are set."

Hearing him say tomorrow startled the hell out of me. I thought I'd have a little time to formulate a plan that'd protect the both of us, but I was wrong.

"Matter of fact, I'm going to go work on that now. I'll link up with you real soon," he said, stepping out of my car.

I nodded in agreement, but as soon as he hopped in his car and drove past me, I dropped my head onto the steering wheel. I wanted peace, a way out, perhaps any form of help. The burdens I carried were so heavy I was sure I'd fall any second now.

I was in no rush at all to get back to the apartment with Bunz. She appeared abnormally unbothered by mine and Iesha's break up. She acted like she wanted me to sex her, but that was the furthest thing from my mind. I needed to get some of this shit off my chest. I considered my mother, but quickly thought against it. Knowing her love for Maine had always been stronger than the love she had for me, she'd probably behead me if she knew exactly what I was up to. I loved Iesha, but telling her all the facts could result in her telling on me to save herself. Other than those two, there was one more person: Jaelyn. It bothered me that I couldn't rap with him. I wouldn't tell him everything but his presence would surely fill the void of loneliness. I felt as if my back was against the ropes and whichever route I chose, I was fucked.

Ah'Million

***

The lights in the living room were dim as I entered the apartment Iesha and I once shared.

"Bunz!" I called out. I wanted to inform her that the entire transaction would go down tomorrow once I received the call from Maine. I peered around for Bunz, but she wasn't anywhere in sight. She could only be in one or two places: the sofa or the restroom. Since she wasn't on the sofa, I checked the restroom, but it was empty also. I was beginning to think Bunz was gone until I opened the door to my bedroom and spotted both her and Iesha naked as the day they came from their mother's wombs. They were so into it they didn't hear or see me enter. The strap that I had used a hundred times to penetrate Iesha, Bunz wore it as she stroked her long and hard from the back. With each thrust, her butt cheeks tightened and Iesha's moans grew louder.

"Cum for me, bitch!" Bunz yelled after slapping Iesha on the ass cheek.

Iesha was positioned at the edge of the bed on all fours. My chest tightened as the beat of my heart quickened. I was furious. Everything that had taken place, and now this. I pulled the Desert Eagle from my waist and swiftly crept up behind Bunz, yanking her head back by the extremely long bundles, ceasing her movements.

I fired into the side of her face. Chunks of Bunz's flesh and blood went flying in every direction. Iesha turned around, alarmed, staring at the barrel of the Desert Eagle that I held so close to her face. The warm tears burned my sockets as they fell down my cheeks.

"Bre'untae it's, it's not what——"

"Say less, Iesha. It's cool. I knew you were bound to do some fuck shit the day you were released from prison."

"That's a lie, Tae. You, you fucked me over," she argued, turning around to face me. Sweat from their love session sweat still decorated her forehead.

146

I peered at her in disgust as she inched closer. Smelling pussy on her breath, I stepped back and fired three shots into her body. Two tore through her chest and one in her stomach.

The sirens could be heard faintly. There was no doubt they were on the way. I looked around the room. There was no time to grab anything. There wasn't anything that significant to grab. My mind was in a frenzy. I didn't know if I should hide the bodies, hide the gun, or start bleaching shit.

"Fuck it," I spoke aloud, jogging towards the front door.

I slung the door open to find multiple cop cars parked outside beneath my apartment in the semi-empty lot. The sight was so terrifying, it almost made me shit my pants. I rushed back inside to face reality. I could either go out blazing, or spend the rest of my life in prison for the two lifeless bodies inside the bedroom. Images of Jaelyn, my mother, Maine, and even Syren flashed inside my head. The last thing I wanted was to leave, but I had to go.

"Lord forgive me," I prayed right before jamming the barrel of the gun inside my mouth.

Boom!

Maine

"Pick up the phone, Tae," I mumbled as I listened to the other end of the phone ring. I sat in my car with the phone pressed against my ear in hopes of hearing Tae's voice.

Shit was definitely real. Not only were the Feds trying to pin my ex-best friend's body on me, I also had no clue where Jaelyn had run off to. A part of me believed he was hiding out at Monty's, but after switching up my car and watching his house from a distance for a few days, I assumed he was telling the truth. Regretting my actions, I simply wanted to reach out and make it up to him not in a sense of apologizing. Not only was I too prideful for that but, I truly wasn't sorry. I just regretted the way I did it. I shouldn't've been as harsh. The fact of the matter remained that I was not in agreeance with nor would I accept his lifestyle.

"Fuck it," I spoke aloud and headed into the opposite direction. I was so spooked. Yesterday I fired Jerry and shut the club down. A night like tonight Mack City would be jumping, but as I veered into the empty lot, it was everything but that.

Syren

I found it rather disturbing that I hadn't heard from Symphony in nearly three weeks. Jaelyn still hadn't admitted to what exactly happened to him. I hadn't had a good night's rest since then. Since I picked him up from his friend's house, he and I had been at Sir'Mahd's home. He and Amyah had gotten so close in only a matter of days. I cooked, cleaned, fucked, and sucked the life out of Sir'Mahd to simply show gratitude and appreciation. He was amazing. I could lie down and wake up to him forever, but before I could focus solely on true happiness and the future, I had to handle this demon from the past. A part of me believed it was Maine's fault. He could've possibly gotten himself in some sort of drama and his enemies targeted Jaelyn because I could never imagine Maine doing it to Jaelyn himself. I tried contacting Maine, but he constantly forwarded my calls.

Logging onto my Instagram, I decided I'd just message him and see what happened. I scrolled down my news feed, instantly spotting things that indicated Tae was deceased. My eyes bucked in disbelief and for seconds, I stopped breathing. I scrolled to Tae's page and quickly scanned everything in awe. Tears welled up in my eyes as sorrow consumes me. I hadn't spoken to Tae in a little while, but there was no doubting my love for her.

"Jaelyn!" I yelled. I hated to be the bearer of bad news but I had to, knowing how greatly he'd been trying to contact him lately.

"Yes ma'am?" he asked, rushing inside of my bedroom cheerfully.

"Yes ma'am me too," Amyah joined in right behind him. I decided to tell him the news in front of Amyah. He might need support from the both of us.

"Baby, I have something to tell you," I spoke in a low and serious tone.

He scanned my face noticing the tears. "Momma, what's wrong?"

"Babe, Tae passed."

"No, uh-uh, Momma, Tae is too young to pass," he said, disallowing the allegations. He shook his head as he attempted to smile, but with each passing second, the smile faded.

"She committed suicide," I added.

"No!" Jaelyn wailed, falling to his knees.

Amyah wrapped her arms around his neck in an attempt to console him. I climbed out of bed and I held him as well.

"She can't leave me, Momma. I love Aunty Tae. She's the only one that truly understands me. She's my confidant, my best friend. NO!" he cried through sniffles nearly choking on his tears.

I tried to decipher exactly what he meant, but at the moment, it was difficult.

"She didn't kill herself. She'd never do that. That evil sack of shit father of mine did this!" he yelled, wrinkles formed across my forehead because now I was confused yet, I was attentive.

"Why would your father hurt Tae?"

"He would! Just like he hurt me because he thinks I'm a queer. Maybe I am, I don't know. All my life I did everything so that I'd be the best son. I even hid my emotions from you. I was distant towards you so that I could appease him and it still wasn't enough. Telling me I shouldn't do this or that 'cause it was considered gay. I hate him!"

Furious was an understatement. I bit down on the corner of my lip. My heart was beating like a drum and I was ready to body Maine's ass. All this time I thought something was mentally wrong or he was simply upset with me, but all along it was Maine's ass. "Are you serious, Jaelyn?"

"Ye-yes ma'am. I'm sorry, Momma."

"So why exactly did he beat you?" I asked curiously.

"He caught me watching a sex movie with gay men." He looked at me shamefully.

"Don't be too afraid to tell me anything. What you prefer is your choice. Fuck him!" I yelled. I couldn't wait to tell Sir'Mahd.

***

When I heard the front door slam, I ran out of the bedroom and into the front room. Shockingly, I saw my mother in the center of the living room, looking around.

"Momma!" I yelled, hugging her tightly.

"Hey baby," she spoke joyfully.

"Jaelyn, Amyah!"

As the two of them embraced my mother, I stand beside Sir'Mahd intertwining my hand with his. Amyah hugged and welcomed my mother as if she'd known her, her entire life. She was truly an angel.

"Show her around," Sir'Mahd voiced, which was perfect because I needed to speak with him.

***

"There it is," I whispered, pointing at Maine's black and blue Dodge Challenger. I had no clue of his whereabouts. I'd given Sir'Mahd the directions to his club in hopes he'd be here, and he was. The lot was dark and deserted .

"You know, all this time I didn't dawn on me that your ex-dude was Maine. Now everything is coming back to me. I was in the club that night shooting pool when he kicked you out," he admitted.

"Indeed you were," I said, smiling as I reflected back on that night.

"I wanted you then."

Laughing at the irony of it all, we leaned in for a kiss before parking in a spot closest to the door.

"How will we get in?" I asked.

"Don't worry 'bout that. I got that."

Sir'Mahd reversed out of the parking spot and drove towards the side, parking alongside the building. He twisted an additional piece of metal onto the barrel of the gun.

"I want you to go to his car so that'll activate his alarm, but don't move just stay there."

"Stay there?" I asked, confused.

"Yeah, trust me. I got you," he assured, staring deeply into my eyes. At the same time we leaned in for a kiss – a long and passionate kiss that I didn't want to end.

"Come on, mama. If we gon' handle this, we got to move now."

I cupped his chin, giving him one more peck before hopping out of the truck. I strutted towards Maine's car and once I was close enough, I hit the window with the palm of my hand.

Beep! Beep! Beep! Beep! Beep!

Immediately I spotted Maine peeking out the door. Once he realized it was me, he rushed outside. Terror consumed me, but it went away once he began to speak.

"Syren, it's not what you think. I know you're upset with me, but he pissed me off and I simply punished him."

"Motherfucker, you went too far.'

"I did, and I'm sorry. Baby, I'm in some shit, deep shit, and right now I ne——"

Psst! Psst! Psst! Psst!

Maine's body jerked as each bullet tore through his flesh. I stared at him in awe as he lost consciousness. I was certainly upset, but hearing and seeing him so troubled surely bothered me. I was stunned as he dropped in front of me.

"Syren! Come on!" Sir'Mahd yelled, but I was in some sort of trance. "Let's go!" he called out once more.

I rushed to the car as if I was being chased while Sir'Mahd swerved out of the lot.

***

Once Sir'Mahd and I arrived home, we burnt the clothes we wore and showered. At one point I wrapped my arms around his waist as the water descended down my back. He picked me up and I wrapped my legs around his waist.

"Don't worry, mama I got you. You just keep tonight between the two of us and we going to be good. Me, you, your moms, Jaelyn, and Amyah," he assured me right before kissing my lips.

For nearly an hour he slowly and sweetly deep stroked my kitty until I was weak as an eighty-year-old woman.

The next day I awoke to several missed calls from Symphony. A part of me was upset at her, but I was so happy to hear from my only friend.

"Hey bae, you mind if Symphony comes over?" I asked Sir'Mahd as soon as he entered the room.

"What I tell you about that Sy? This our shit," he said, appearing a bit frustrated.

"It's cool anyways 'cause I'm taking the kids to the mall today."

"Okay. Where's Mom?"

"Down in the den watching LMN."

"Okay. I still can't believe you went to get her for me."

"I love you, Sy."

"I love you too, bae," I responded, giddy as a child.

"Look at us! " Amyah yelled, bursting into the room.

They were dressed flamboyantly in runway attire. They both pretended to be models in front of a famous photographer. Amyah dressed feminine and Jaelyn masculine. They looked like teen professionals.

***

"Hey bitch!" I greeted as soon as I opened the door for Symphony. Dressed in a burgundy and cream long-sleeved Timberland shirt, light denim jeans, and matching Timberlands, Symphony wrapped her arms around my neck, entering my home. She glowed immensely. I didn't know if it was the face beat or if the glow was natural.

"I got something for you," she said, pulling the purple box out of her Hermes bag. I was a sucker for surprises.

"What is it?" I asked, balling my fist in excitement.

As soon as she handed me the purple box, I forced it open. The gold and pink diamond-encrusted Rolex watch was impeccably beautiful. I stared in awe before squeezing Symphony tightly. The Rolex made me forget about her vanishing for weeks. Knowing how expensive the piece of jewelry was, I questioned her as if she was a culprit in an interrogation room. Symphony and I laughed, had drinks, and reminisced about the old times until she decided to go.

Six months later

"Basketball player!" Jaelyn yelled. "NBA player," he continued.

"No, no, keep guessing!" Sir'Mahd shouted.

"Oh, oh, Lebron James!"

"Got it!"

The four of us played charades while my mother watched, closely reclined in the love seat. Amyah and I were on a team, and Jaelyn and Sir'Mahd were a team. Jaelyn and Sir'Mahd were merely a point ahead when a knock so loud that it could be heard throughout the house came from the front door. We all looked around confused. No one had been expected.

I glanced at Sir'Mahd.

"Just chill," he whispered before answering the door.

As soon as the locks were undone, police came flying in with guns drawn.

"Put those guns down. It's kids in here!" I yelled as tears blurred my vision.

"What's the problem, officers?" Sir'Mahd voiced loudly, appearing calm as possible

One of the officers jerked him roughly before cuffing him.

"Who's Syren Wiley?"

"I am," I spoke weakly.

They pressed my face against the wall. I was cuffed and dragged out of my home. They threw Sir'Mahd and I into separate vehicles before taking us into custody.

What is this about? I thought, hoping it was anything other than what I assumed, but my gut never let me astray. Luckily, Sir'Mahd and I ended up in book-in together. We sat at a distance, but we were still able to communicate. I wanted to be strong so I wouldn't stress Sir'Mahd, but I could see the pain and distress in his eyes after noticing my tear-stained cheeks.

"I got you. Just stay quiet. I got you," he mouthed.

After reading his lips, I felt a sense of relief. Since meeting Sir'Mahd, everything he ever promised was delivered.

"Syren Wiley!" the officer yelled.

I looked back at him then cut my eyes at Sir'Mahd before walking to the desk. "Sir?" I asked timidly.

"We need to take your mugshot. Stand over there behind that counter."

"May I ask what I'm being charged with?"

"First degree murder."

Although my heart fell to my feet, I pretended to be unbothered. I didn't utter another word to the officer. I simply followed the instructions given and returned to my seat.

"They got us for murder," I mouthed to Sir'Mahd before taking a seat.

"We knew this day could possibly come. It's okay."

I shook my head in disbelief, hoping he was right. Sir'Mahd was called to the desk next. I listened closely as the officer rambled off the same thing to him as he did to me.

"We gon' make bond and go from there. Just chill, mama. I ain't left yet. I'm surely not gon' leave you hanging now," he whispered as he walked past me.

Sir'Mahd's strength was one of the main things I fell for upon meeting him. Two officers bent the corrner and led Sir'Mahd and I upstairs. Inside the elevator, our lips locked like magnets.

"Hey, cut that shit out!" the white male officer yelled.

"Fuck you! Lock me up!" Sir'Mahd blurted.

I didn't know what would happen next. I was afraid of things becoming any worse.

The four of us entered the small courtroom for magistrate court, I wasn't truly worried about the bond amount. Whatever the cost was, Sir'Mahd could handle it.

One at a time we were called forward just to hear the judge say, "No bond will be set at this time," before the gavel banged.

Anxiety arose and the confidence I once had vanished like urine in a pool. Terror and negativity consumed me like a wild fire and instantly I became dizzy.

"Mama, just chill. I'm going to get us the best attorney money can buy. This some bullshit!" I heard Sir'Mahd scream before everything went black.

Several months later

"Ms. Wiley, court is in session in ten minutes. Just remember everything we rehearsed and you'll walk out today a free woman," my attorney, Mr. Jenkins, assured me.

Sir'Mahd had come up with the idea for me to testify against him to obtain a chance at freedom. At the beginning of our arrest he attempted to file an affidavit admitting I had no dealings with Maine's murder and it was solely on him, but it was useless since I was placed at the murder, automatically labelling me as a accessory. In the state of Texas, accessory laws do not exist. Therefore, I received the same charge as Sir'Mahd. Although so much was on the line, Sir'Mahd remained optimistic about things, adeptly hiding his fears. Sir'Mahd felt as if there was no sense in the both of us doing time, so he came up with the idea to capitalize on the opportunity. I'd agree to take the stand and tell the judge, the district attorney, and whomever else was present what they actually already knew. Assuming the authorities lacked evidence, both Sir'Mahd and I quickly found out there was an informant who had enough information to compel the charges to stick - an informant that Sir'Mahd and myself hoped our lawyers would discredit.

"Mr. Jenkins, what happens if we lose?"

"We? You mean your boyfriend. He is going to lose so you can win."

"Well, ye-yes."

"Ninety-nine years in prison Ms. Wiley," he spoke firmly.

The thought of all that time hit me suddenly and harshly like a bee sting. I was hoping I'd at least see Symphony in attendance, although I hadn't heard much from her after I was informed she'd gotten herself into a bit of a jam.

"Will I take the stand before or after the informant?"

"After. Matter of fact, it's time," he announced, peering down at his watch.

Mr. Jenkins and I were led into the courtroom by an officer. As soon as the door opened, I scanned the area quickly. Just as I hoped I would, I spotted Symphony, who was sitting beside Draco on the bench. Although I hadn't seen or spoke to Draco since the night of King's birthday party, she still showed up when I needed her.

Jaelyn, Amyah, and my mother waved cheerfully. Only Lord knew how much I would miss them. At sixteen knocking on seventeen, Jaelyn was my go-to. He handled whatever needed to be taken care of between both Sir'Mahd and me.

Enthused, I waved back. The sight of them alone made me tear up. The door to the opposite side of the courtroom opened and Sir'Mahd walked in. For a second, everything ceased. The movement, the chatter, the typing sound from the clerk, and the jingling of the officer's keys. I'd last seen Sir'Mahd several months ago at book-in. He was more appealing than before. The light beard made him appear a few years older, but it was enticing. Outwardly he was the same ole tough Sir'Mahd, but inwardly, he was decaying once spotting Amyah and myself. He hurriedly blinked away the tears that began to form in his eyes, but not before I saw them. Seeing him made me realize how much I missed him, and all I could do was stare in awe.

"I love you," I mouthed.

"I love you too."

"The state of Texas vs. Sir'Mahd Kingsley." After the D.A. stated the obvious, he announced, "I'd like to call my first witness to the stand. Symphony Jacobs."

I peered back at Symphony, confused, as my heart raced in terror. I was so busy with my mother and kids I didn't notice that Symphony and Draco were sitting on the opposite side of the courtroom. Neither of them would look me in the eye. Enraged, I envisioned myself whooping both of their asses. I was anxious to hear what Symphony had to say because I didn't recall telling her shit.

"Ms. Jacobs, start from the beginning."

Sir Mahd cut his eyes at me, dumbfounded. I returned his glance with a hint of nervousness as I shrugged my shoulders.

"Well, I hadn't seen Syren in about two to three weeks, so I went to visit her and Sir'Mahd at his new home. After giving her a present, we sat down and had drinks. Well, after a few shots of tequila, we both began to ramble about what had taken place in the last two to three weeks."

Hearing Symphony recall the past events, I suddenly remembered that day clearly. Shameful and blameworthy, I lowered my head. *How could I be so careless?* I thought. Ra'Keisha's letter tried to warn me, but I refused to take heed.

"Thank you, Ms. Jacobs," the D.A. announced as Symphony descended the steps, using the Kleenex to dry her eyes.

"Ole fake-ass bitch," I voiced loud enough to hear. She kept walking as if she didn't hear me and sat next to Draco, who kissed her on the forehead and held her close.

"What the fuck? They're together?" I asked in disbelief.

This shit cant get any more interesting, I thought.

"I would like to call my witness, Ms. Wiley, to the stand."

I took a seat on the stand, peering at everyone in the room. My eyes lingered on my family, then Sir'Mahd.

"Ms. Wiley, what happened on the night of July 26th, 2019?" he asked after I agreed to the oath.

"I don't know. Ask that bitch," I responded, shocking half the courtroom. Sir'Mahd's eyes were as big as golf balls.

"Ms. Wiley, calm down. Now tell me what happened——"

"I just told you, and that's all I have to say," I said, cutting him short.

"Judge Dunn, can I please have a word with my client?"

"Five minutes, Mr. Jenkins."

"Syren, what are you doing? This is your life on the line here!" he spoke loudly through clenched teeth.

"Fuck you and the motherfuckas you're working with. Give me my time," I spoke loud enough where anyone who was paying attention could hear. In one simple gesture, he directed me to my seat.

"What's wrong with you, Syren?" Sir'Mahd asked as I bypassed him.

"We in this together," I simply replied, teary-eyed.

"But what about the——"

"They gon' be fine. Jaelyn has access to the accounts. It's plenty of money in there. I could never do that to you. I love you, Sir'Mahd."

"But that was the plan," he shot back.

"Well, change of plans. It's levels to this shit. We gon' weather this storm together."

The End

Submission Guideline

Submit the first three chapters of your completed manuscript to ldpsubmissions@gmail.com, subject line: Your book's title. The manuscript must be in a .doc file and sent as an attachment. Document should be in Times New Roman, double spaced and in size 12 font. Also, provide your synopsis and full contact information. If sending multiple submissions, they must each be in a separate email.

Have a story but no way to send it electronically? You can still submit to LDP/Ca$h Presents. Send in the first three chapters, written or typed, of your completed manuscript to:

LDP: Submissions Dept
Po Box 944
Stockbridge, Ga 30281

DO NOT send original manuscript. Must be a duplicate.

Provide your synopsis and a cover letter containing your full contact information.

Thanks for considering LDP and Ca$h Presents.

Coming Soon from Lock Down Publications/Ca$h Presents

BOW DOWN TO MY GANGSTA

By **Ca$h**

TORN BETWEEN TWO

By **Coffee**

THE STREETS STAINED MY SOUL **II**

By **Marcellus Allen**

BLOOD OF A BOSS **VI**

SHADOWS OF THE GAME II

TRAP BASTARD II

By **Askari**

LOYAL TO THE GAME **IV**

By **T.J. & Jelissa**

IF LOVING YOU IS WRONG… **III**

By **Jelissa**

TRUE SAVAGE **VIII**

MIDNIGHT CARTEL IV

DOPE BOY MAGIC IV

CITY OF KINGZ III

By **Chris Green**

BLAST FOR ME **III**

A SAVAGE DOPEBOY III

CUTTHROAT MAFIA III

DUFFLE BAG CARTEL VI

HEARTLESS GOON VI

By **Ghost**

A HUSTLER'S DECEIT III

KILL ZONE **II**

BAE BELONGS TO ME III

A DOPE BOY'S QUEEN III

By **Aryanna**

COKE KINGS V

KING OF THE TRAP III

By **T.J. Edwards**

GORILLAZ IN THE BAY V

3X KRAZY III

De'Kari

THE STREETS ARE CALLING II

Duquie Wilson

KINGPIN KILLAZ IV

STREET KINGS III

PAID IN BLOOD III

CARTEL KILLAZ IV

DOPE GODS III

Hood Rich

SINS OF A HUSTLA II

ASAD

KINGZ OF THE GAME VI

Playa Ray

SLAUGHTER GANG IV

RUTHLESS HEART IV

By **Willie Slaughter**

FUK SHYT II

By Blakk Diamond

TRAP QUEEN

RICH $AVAGE II

By Troublesome

YAYO V

GHOST MOB II

Stilloan Robinson

CREAM III

By Yolanda Moore

SON OF A DOPE FIEND III

HEAVEN GOT A GHETTO II

By Renta

FOREVER GANGSTA II

GLOCKS ON SATIN SHEETS III

By Adrian Dulan

LOYALTY AIN'T PROMISED III

By Keith Williams

THE PRICE YOU PAY FOR LOVE III

By Destiny Skai

I'M NOTHING WITHOUT HIS LOVE II

SINS OF A THUG II

By Monet Dragun

LIFE OF A SAVAGE IV

MURDA SEASON IV

GANGLAND CARTEL IV

CHI'RAQ GANGSTAS IV

KILLERS ON ELM STREET III

JACK BOYZ N DA BRONX II

A DOPEBOY'S DREAM II

By **Romell Tukes**

QUIET MONEY IV

EXTENDED CLIP III

THUG LIFE IV

By **Trai'Quan**

THE STREETS MADE ME III

By **Larry D. Wright**

IF YOU CROSS ME ONCE II

ANGEL III

By **Anthony Fields**

FRIEND OR FOE III

By **Mimi**

SAVAGE STORMS III

By **Meesha**

BLOOD ON THE MONEY III

By J-Blunt

THE STREETS WILL NEVER CLOSE II

By K'ajji

NIGHTMARES OF A HUSTLA III

By King Dream

IN THE ARM OF HIS BOSS

By Jamila

MONEY, MURDER & MEMORIES III

Malik D. Rice

CONCRETE KILLAZ II

Ah'Million

By Kingpen
HARD AND RUTHLESS II
By Von Wiley Hall
MOB TIES III
By SayNoMore
BODYMORE MURDERLAND II
By Delmont Player
THE LAST OF THE OGS III
Tranay Adams
FOR THE LOVE OF A BOSS II
By C. D. Blue

Available Now

RESTRAINING ORDER **I & II**
By **CA$H & Coffee**
LOVE KNOWS NO BOUNDARIES **I II & III**
By **Coffee**
RAISED AS A GOON I, II, III & IV
BRED BY THE SLUMS I, II, III
BLAST FOR ME I & II
ROTTEN TO THE CORE I II III
A BRONX TALE I, II, III
DUFFLE BAG CARTEL I II III IV V
HEARTLESS GOON I II III IV V

A SAVAGE DOPEBOY I II

DRUG LORDS I II III

CUTTHROAT MAFIA I II

By **Ghost**

LAY IT DOWN **I & II**

LAST OF A DYING BREED I II

BLOOD STAINS OF A SHOTTA I & II III

By **Jamaica**

LOYAL TO THE GAME I II III

LIFE OF SIN I, II III

By **TJ & Jelissa**

BLOODY COMMAS I & II

SKI MASK CARTEL I II & III

KING OF NEW YORK I II,III IV V

RISE TO POWER I II III

COKE KINGS I II III IV

BORN HEARTLESS I II III IV

KING OF THE TRAP I II

By **T.J. Edwards**

IF LOVING HIM IS WRONG…I & II

LOVE ME EVEN WHEN IT HURTS I II III

By **Jelissa**

WHEN THE STREETS CLAP BACK I & II III

THE HEART OF A SAVAGE I II III

By **Jibril Williams**

A DISTINGUISHED THUG STOLE MY HEART I II & III

LOVE SHOULDN'T HURT I II III IV

RENEGADE BOYS I II III IV

PAID IN KARMA I II III

SAVAGE STORMS I II

By **Meesha**

A GANGSTER'S CODE I &, II III

A GANGSTER'S SYN I II III

THE SAVAGE LIFE I II III

CHAINED TO THE STREETS I II III

BLOOD ON THE MONEY I II

By J-Blunt

PUSH IT TO THE LIMIT

By **Bre' Hayes**

BLOOD OF A BOSS **I, II, III, IV, V**

SHADOWS OF THE GAME

TRAP BASTARD

By **Askari**

THE STREETS BLEED MURDER **I, II & III**

THE HEART OF A GANGSTA I II& III

By **Jerry Jackson**

CUM FOR ME I II III IV V VI VII

An **LDP Erotica Collaboration**

BRIDE OF A HUSTLA **I II & II**

THE FETTI GIRLS **I, II& III**

CORRUPTED BY A GANGSTA I, II III, IV

BLINDED BY HIS LOVE

THE PRICE YOU PAY FOR LOVE I II

DOPE GIRL MAGIC I II III

By **Destiny Skai**

WHEN A GOOD GIRL GOES BAD

By **Adrienne**

THE COST OF LOYALTY I II III

By Kweli

A GANGSTER'S REVENGE **I II III & IV**

THE BOSS MAN'S DAUGHTERS I II III IV V

A SAVAGE LOVE **I & II**

BAE BELONGS TO ME I II

A HUSTLER'S DECEIT I, II, III

WHAT BAD BITCHES DO I, II, III

SOUL OF A MONSTER I II III

KILL ZONE

A DOPE BOY'S QUEEN I II

By **Aryanna**

A KINGPIN'S AMBITON

A KINGPIN'S AMBITION **II**

I MURDER FOR THE DOUGH

By **Ambitious**

TRUE SAVAGE I II III IV V VI VII

DOPE BOY MAGIC I, II, III

MIDNIGHT CARTEL I II III

CITY OF KINGZ I II

By **Chris Green**

A DOPEBOY'S PRAYER

By **Eddie "Wolf" Lee**

THE KING CARTEL **I, II & III**

By **Frank Gresham**

THESE NIGGAS AIN'T LOYAL **I, II & III**

By **Nikki Tee**

GANGSTA SHYT **I II &III**

By **CATO**

THE ULTIMATE BETRAYAL

By **Phoenix**

BOSS'N UP **I , II & III**

By **Royal Nicole**

I LOVE YOU TO DEATH

By Destiny J

I RIDE FOR MY HITTA

I STILL RIDE FOR MY HITTA

By **Misty Holt**

LOVE & CHASIN' PAPER

By **Qay Crockett**

TO DIE IN VAIN

SINS OF A HUSTLA

By **ASAD**

BROOKLYN HUSTLAZ

By **Boogsy Morina**

BROOKLYN ON LOCK I & II

By **Sonovia**

GANGSTA CITY

By **Teddy Duke**

A DRUG KING AND HIS DIAMOND I & II III

A DOPEMAN'S RICHES

HER MAN, MINE'S TOO I, II

CASH MONEY HO'S

THE WIFEY I USED TO BE I II

By Nicole Goosby

TRAPHOUSE KING **I II & III**

KINGPIN KILLAZ I II III

STREET KINGS I II

PAID IN BLOOD **I II**

CARTEL KILLAZ I II III

DOPE GODS I II

By **Hood Rich**

LIPSTICK KILLAH **I, II, III**

CRIME OF PASSION I II & III

FRIEND OR FOE I II

By **Mimi**

STEADY MOBBN' **I, II, III**

THE STREETS STAINED MY SOUL

By **Marcellus Allen**

WHO SHOT YA **I, II, III**

SON OF A DOPE FIEND I II

HEAVEN GOT A GHETTO

Renta

GORILLAZ IN THE BAY **I II III IV**

TEARS OF A GANGSTA I II

3X KRAZY I II

DE'KARI

TRIGGADALE I II III

Elijah R. Freeman

GOD BLESS THE TRAPPERS I, II, III

THESE SCANDALOUS STREETS I, II, III

FEAR MY GANGSTA I, II, III IV, V

THESE STREETS DON'T LOVE NOBODY I, II

BURY ME A G I, II, III, IV, V

A GANGSTA'S EMPIRE I, II, III, IV

THE DOPEMAN'S BODYGAURD I II

THE REALEST KILLAZ I II III

THE LAST OF THE OGS I II

Tranay Adams

THE STREETS ARE CALLING

Duquie Wilson

MARRIED TO A BOSS… I II III

By Destiny Skai & Chris Green

KINGZ OF THE GAME I II III IV V

Playa Ray

SLAUGHTER GANG I II III

RUTHLESS HEART I II III

By Willie Slaughter

FUK SHYT

By Blakk Diamond

DON'T F#CK WITH MY HEART I II

By Linnea

ADDICTED TO THE DRAMA I II III

IN THE ARM OF HIS BOSS II

By Jamila

YAYO I II III IV

A SHOOTER'S AMBITION I II

By S. Allen

TRAP GOD I II III

RICH $AVAGE

By Troublesome

FOREVER GANGSTA

GLOCKS ON SATIN SHEETS I II

By Adrian Dulan

TOE TAGZ I II III

LEVELS TO THIS SHYT

By Ah'Million

KINGPIN DREAMS I II III

By Paper Boi Rari

CONFESSIONS OF A GANGSTA I II III

By Nicholas Lock

I'M NOTHING WITHOUT HIS LOVE

SINS OF A THUG

By Monet Dragun

CAUGHT UP IN THE LIFE I II III

By Robert Baptiste

NEW TO THE GAME I II III

MONEY, MURDER & MEMORIES I II

By **Malik D. Rice**

LIFE OF A SAVAGE I II III

A GANGSTA'S QUR'AN I II III

MURDA SEASON I II III

GANGLAND CARTEL I II III

CHI'RAQ GANGSTAS I II III

KILLERS ON ELM STREET I II

JACK BOYZ N DA BRONX

A DOPEBOY'S DREAM

By **Romell Tukes**

LOYALTY AIN'T PROMISED I II

By Keith Williams

QUIET MONEY I II III

THUG LIFE I II III

EXTENDED CLIP I II

By **Trai'Quan**

THE STREETS MADE ME I II

By **Larry D. Wright**

THE ULTIMATE SACRIFICE I, II, III, IV, V, VI

KHADIFI

IF YOU CROSS ME ONCE

ANGEL I II

By **Anthony Fields**

THE LIFE OF A HOOD STAR

By Ca$h & Rashia Wilson

THE STREETS WILL NEVER CLOSE

By K'ajji

CREAM I II

By Yolanda Moore

NIGHTMARES OF A HUSTLA I II

By King Dream

CONCRETE KILLAZ

By Kingpen

HARD AND RUTHLESS

By Von Wiley Hall

GHOST MOB II

Stilloan Robinson

MOB TIES I II

By SayNoMore

BODYMORE MURDERLAND

By Delmont Player

FOR THE LOVE OF A BOSS

By C. D. Blue

BOOKS BY LDP'S CEO, CA$H

TRUST IN NO MAN

TRUST IN NO MAN 2

TRUST IN NO MAN 3

BONDED BY BLOOD

SHORTY GOT A THUG

THUGS CRY

THUGS CRY 2

THUGS CRY 3

TRUST NO BITCH

TRUST NO BITCH 2

TRUST NO BITCH 3

TIL MY CASKET DROPS

RESTRAINING ORDER

RESTRAINING ORDER 2

IN LOVE WITH A CONVICT

LIFE OF A HOOD STAR